FREDDY

the

PILOT

WALTER R. BROOKS

Illustrated by Kurt Wiese

THE OVERLOOK PRESS
NEW YORK, NY

FREDDY

the PILOT

If you enjoyed this book, very likely you will be interested not only in the other Freddy books published in this series, but also in joining the *Friends of Freddy,* an organization of Freddy devotees.

We will be pleased to hear from any reader about our "Freddy" publishing program. You can easily contact us by logging on to either THE OVERLOOK PRESS website or the Freddy website.

The website addresses are as follows:

THE OVERLOOK PRESS
www.overlookpress.com

FREDDY
www.friendsoffreddy.org

We look forward to hearing from you soon.

This edition first published in paperback in the United States in 2012 by

The Overlook Press, Peter Mayer Publishers, Inc.
141 Wooster Street
New York, NY 10012
www.overlookpress.com
For bulk and special sales, please contact sales@overlookny.com

Library of Congress Cataloging-in-Publication Data

Brooks, Walter R., 1886-1958
Freddy the pilot / Walter R. Brooks ;
illustrated by Kurt Wiese
p. cm.
I. Title.
ISBN 978-1-59020-867-0

Manufactured in the United States of America

2 4 6 8 10 9 7 5 3 1

FREDDY

the

PILOT

CHAPTER

1

Freddy, the pig, was lying on his stomach in the grass beside the duck pond reading a book. It was a hot day and the grass was cool—at least it was cool for about the length of time it took him to read two pages. By that time he would have warmed it up and would have to shift to a fresh spot. So every time he turned a leaf he rolled over once.

He had rolled in this manner about halfway around the pond and about halfway through his story, when a shadow fell across the page and a voice said: "Hi, Freddy. Got any comics to trade?"

Freddy didn't look up. "Begone! Get thee hence!" he said and went on reading.

"Get what?" said the voice. "What you talking about?"

"Oh, gosh!" said Freddy disgustedly, and he closed the book, keeping his finger in the place, and looked up to see Sniffy Wilson, the skunk, sitting beside him. "Oh, it's you, Sniffy," he said. "Well, this book is the story of Robin Hood, and 'Get thee hence,'—well, that's the way they used to talk in his times, hundreds of years ago. It means 'Go away.'"

"Well, why wouldn't they say what they mean?" Sniffy asked. "That's the trouble with books: you have to think what they mean all the time."

Freddy grinned at him. "Yeah," he said. "It's

tough trying to think if you haven't anything to think with."

"Oh, is that so!" retorted the skunk. "Well, I guess I've got just as much brain as you have! Golly, all I did is ask you if you had some comics to trade—"

"Comics!" Freddy interrupted. "Baby stuff! No self-respecting animal over two years old looks at that trash. Oh, go away and quit bothering me. Take your hollow head somewhere else."

From over the edge of the bank, down by the water, came a little flat giggle. Freddy knew that giggle. It belonged to Uncle Wesley, a plump and pompous duck who, with his two nieces, lived beside the pond. Freddy knew, too, that Uncle Wesley never giggled at an ordinary joke; the only thing that amused the duck was when somebody said something mean or sarcastic. And he didn't want to say mean things to Sniffy, who was a good friend.

So before the skunk could answer, he said, "I beg your pardon, Sniffy. I don't really mean that, of course. It's just that I think these comics are foolish. I don't see how anybody can look at them when there are so many books around that are more interesting."

"Yeah?" said Sniffy grumpily. "Such as that old thing you're reading, I suppose!"

Freddy didn't answer directly. "This Robin Hood was quite a guy," he said. "He was an outlaw and he hid out in Sherwood forest with his band of men. They'd send out soldiers to catch him but he'd play some trick on them and get away. And he'd disguise himself and go to a fair and walk off with the prize for shooting right under the sheriff's nose. Or he'd take on all comers at a bout with quarterstaves."

"With what?" Sniffy asked.

"Before they had boxing matches, they used to fight with them," Freddy said. "A quarterstaff was a good stout stick about eight feet long. You held it in the middle, and you could rap with either end. And when the other fellow swung at you, you had to parry,—catch his blows on the end or the middle of your stick. It was awful fast fighting. The sticks would rattle together for a few seconds, and then pop! somebody would get it on the arm or the head. Look, here's a picture—Robin and the sheriff's cook. Robin licked him, and then he joined the band."

Sniffy was poring over the picture when Freddy raised his head. "What's that—thunder?" he asked.

"He's got a sword on," said Sniffy. "Why didn't they fight with swords?"

Freddy didn't answer. He was listening to the sound, which at first hardly more than a vibration of the air, now came more clearly. It was too regular for thunder.

"Would you let me take this book, Freddy?" Sniffy asked.

"The book? Sure, take it along, I've read it three or four times," said Freddy. "I'm just wondering if that sound is what I think it is."

Sniffy listened for a second. "Sounds like guns," he said. "Maybe there's a battle. Maybe the Martians have landed!"

"Oh, golly, you and your comics!" said Freddy. "Hey, Wesley," he called, going to the edge of the bank. "Tell Alice and Emma to come down to the gate. I think we've got important company." And he turned and ran down towards the barnyard.

Some of the other animals had heard that sound too, and they were trooping out of the gate into the road. Nothing could be seen yet,

Sniffy listened for a second.

but the regular boom, boom of a drum could now be heard, and then way off down the road something was moving, there were spots of color, and all at once a brass band broke into the old familiar marching song.

Red and gold wagons are coming down the street,
With a Boomschmidt, Boomschmidt, boom, boom, boom! . . .

"It's the circus!" Mrs. Bean had come out on the front porch. "Come out here, Mr. B. It's Mr. Boomschmidt's circus!"

Always when the circus came to Centerboro, it made a special detour to parade up the road past the Bean farm, where Mr. Boomschmidt and his animals had so many good friends. It always marched in the same order. First, in a loud checked suit and a silk hat—Mr. Boomschmidt himself on his horse, Rod. Then Mr. Boomschmidt's personal car—a large red limousine, trimmed with gold, and with a B in gold, surmounted by a crown, on the door panels. In the car rode Mr. Boomschmidt's mother, and Madame Delphine, the fortune teller. Beside it rode Mademoiselle Rose, the bareback rider (or "equestrienne" as they called her on the posters), on Dexter, her trick horse. Then came the big bandwagon, and then all the animals, two by two, with Bill Wonks and the other circus men riding on the elephants and camels.

The wagons followed along behind, because Mr. Boomschmidt didn't believe in keeping his animals locked up. The animals just used the cages to sleep in. In towns that they'd never visited before, people were quite surprised to see tigers and wolves and hyenas and rhinoceroses walking along in the procession, and some of the more timid were scared. But as a matter of fact the animals were usually a lot better behaved than the onlookers, who sometimes threw pop bottles at the rhinoceros, or poked the lion with umbrellas to see if he'd roar.

The parade marched right in the Bean gate and twice around the barnyard, and then Mr. Boomschmidt took his silk hat and waved it and the band stopped playing, and then he waved the hat again and led the whole circus in the chorus of their marching song. The farm animals knew it, and they all joined in.

BOOM—*be quick! Buy a ticket at the wicket.*
BOOM—*get your pink lemonade; get your gum.*
BOOM—*get your peanuts, popcorn, lollipops.*
BOOM—*Mr. Boom—Mr. Boomschmidt's come!*

After that Mr. Boomschmidt led the circus in three cheers for the Bean farm, and Mr. Bean led his animals in three cheers for the circus, and then the two groups rushed at each other and shook hands and paws and slapped backs, and there was a general uproar and rejoicing.

"You're up this way a little earlier than usual, aren't you, Mr. Boom?" Mrs. Bean asked.

"Yes, we usually don't hit York State till August," Mr. Boomschmidt said. "But we ran into a little trouble on our way north—my gracious, trouble isn't the word for it!" He paused and looked thoughtful. "I wonder what the word for it is? Leo, what would the word for it be? Leo— Oh, my goodness, where are you, Leo?"

Leo, the lion, was just greeting his old friend, Freddy. He turned towards his employer. "Word for what, chief?"

"What we're in. I said trouble wasn't the word for it, but I don't know what the word for it is."

"Dilemma," said the lion. "That's what you said last night we were in—a dilemma."

"Gracious!" said Mr. Boomschmidt. "Sounds awful, doesn't it? What's it mean?"

"It's your word, not mine," said Leo.

Mr. Bean took the pipe out of his mouth. "Same as a quandary," he said, and put the pipe back.

"A quandary," said Mr. Boomschmidt thoughtfully. "Ah yes, quite right—a quandary. Well, Leo . . ."

"It's a bird, I think, chief," said the lion. "Kind of a cross between a swan and a cassowary. Lives in Africa. My Uncle Ajax used to tell me stories about the flocks of wild quandaries on Lake Nyassa—"

Mr. Bean took his pipe out again. "When there's several things you can do, but they're all likely to turn out badly, and you can't decide—you're in a dilemma. You're also in a quandary." He put the pipe back.

Even Mrs. Bean was startled at this display of learning. Mr. Boomschmidt was delighted. "That's it!" he exclaimed. "That's why we're here. We're in a dilemma and a quandary both, and we need an awful good detective to get us out of 'em."

"Well now," said Mrs. Bean, "If you and your mother and Madame Delphine will come in and have a cup of tea—and maybe, Mr. B.," she said to her husband, "you can scratch up some refreshments for these animals." She looked rather doubtfully at the elephants and the tigers and the camels and the rhinoceros, but Mr. Boomschmidt said: "That's awful kind of you, ma'am, but we can't stop now. Have to get over to Centerboro and get the tents up before dark. Perhaps we can come to tea after tomorrow's show."

"If there is a show," Rod muttered.

"Oh, don't be so gloomy," said Mr. Boomschmidt. "My gracious, just because we're in a dilemma now doesn't mean we have to stay in it till next Christmas. Does it, Leo? Goodness, don't just stand there, Leo. Say something cheerful."

"You say it, chief," said Leo. "I'm fresh out of cheerfulness. By next Christmas I'll probably be living in the Old Lions' Home."

"Oh, I guess things won't be as bad as that,"

said Mrs. Bean. "This dilemma you spoke of—"

"It's a snorter," said Mr. Boomschmidt. "Oh, my goodness, I should say so! Yes ma'am, if you want to see a first class, high-powered dilemma in action, you come to tomorrow's show. And you come too, Freddy—you and your partner, Mrs. Wiggins. I've got to have the best detective talent in the country on this thing. That's why we've come straight up to Centerboro. I hope you're free to take a big case?"

The detective firm of Frederick & Wiggins was well and favorably known throughout the entire state. They were a splendid team. Freddy supplied the ideas and Mrs. Wiggins, the cow, supplied the common sense, without which ideas aren't much good. And they had worked for Mr. Boomschmidt before; he knew that he was getting the best talent that money could buy.

"You turn your dilemma over to us," Freddy said. "We'll drop everything else and go right at it."

So it was settled that all the Bean animals would come to the show the following afternoon. Mr. Boomschmidt pulled a pack of tickets out of his pocket and gave one to every animal in the barnyard. And then the parade formed up again and marched off down the road.

Freddy walked over to the cow barn with Mrs. Wiggins.

"Why did you say we'd drop everything else to work on his case, Freddy?" the cow asked. "You know we haven't had a job in the last six weeks."

"Sounds better," said the pig. "And Mr. Boom's an old friend; if we did have any other job we'd drop it, wouldn't we?"

"Land sakes, of course we would. But how can we drop—"

"O K, O K," Freddy interrupted. "So if we've got to drop something, we'll drop all the cases we haven't got. Does that suit you?"

"Sometimes I just don't know what you're talking about," said Mrs. Wiggins.

CHAPTER
2

Boomschmidt's Stupendous and Unexcelled Circus (formerly Boomschmidt's Colossal and Unparalleled Circus) was a little different from most small circuses. For almost all the performers were animals. Mr. Boomschmidt had been smart enough to realize that monkeys can do much more startling feats on trapezes than even the most skilful acrobats can, and that a small rabbit putting lions and tigers through their tricks seems much more daring than a regular lion tamer. His clowns weren't men; they were pandas and kangaroos. And nearly all the circus work—putting up the tents and so on—was done by animals too. Two of the elephants could even swing sledge hammers in their trunks, to drive the pegs to which the tents' guy ropes were fastened.

The only performer who was not an animal was Mademoiselle Rose. People sometimes asked Mr. Boomschmidt why, in an all-animal show, he kept her on. Couldn't he train an animal to do bareback stunts? Mr. Boomschmidt said yes, of course he could, but at least a third of the people who came to his shows came to see Mademoiselle Rose. This was certainly true. Every circus has bareback riders, but Mademoiselle Rose was so pretty, and she did the most daring feats so easily and gracefully, that she was one of the most popular figures in the whole country. And while there are plenty of riders who can stand on their heads on the back of a galloping horse, you can count on the fingers of one hand those who can do it on the back of a galloping rhinoceros. But Mademoiselle Rose did it, at every performance.

Mr. Boomschmidt knew of course that Mademoiselle Rose would not always be with the circus. Some day she would marry one of her many admirers, and the Stupendous and Unexcelled Circus would not be as stupendous and unexcelled as it had been. Not by a good deal. On that day his audiences would be only about half as big as they were today. He hated to think of it. And so, very sensibly, he didn't.

Until Mr. Watson P. Condiment began paying court to Mademoiselle Rose. Then he had to think of it.

Not that Mademoiselle Rose had any intention of marrying Mr. Condiment. She didn't want to live in any of his six big houses, or ride in any of his fifteen big cars, or sail across the ocean in his big yacht. She didn't like Mr. Condiment. Even when he got down on his knees and said: "Please marry me," she just said: "No thank you. Please go away." For she was always polite, even to people she didn't like. And Mr.

Condiment would go. But he always came back in a little while.

Mr. Condiment was a tall thin man who always looked as if he had a stomach ache. That was because he did have a stomach ache. He also had a great deal of money. If people didn't do what he wanted them to he got mad and blustered. But he didn't bluster at Mademoiselle Rose because when he started to, she just turned her back and walked away. He blustered at Mr. Boomschmidt, though. For he had tried to buy the circus, and when Mr. Boomschmidt refused to sell, he got mad. He had figured that if he owned the circus, he would fire Mademoiselle Rose and her mother, Madame Delphine, and then Mademoiselle Rose wouldn't have any money to live on and would have to marry him. But although he offered enormous sums, Mr. Boomschmidt said no. "Very well," Mr. Condiment had said. "You wait. You just wait."

Freddy, of course, hadn't been told anything about this when he and his friends walked down to the Centerboro Fair Grounds that afternoon to see the show. Led by Mr. and Mrs. Bean, the animals had marched in through the gate and into the big tent, where they had been shown to seats in the front row by the usher, a young alligator named Leslie. "I thought I'd come and sit with you when the show begins," he said to them, "but the boss wants me to stay on the job in case there's a panic in the audience."

"Land sakes, I do hope there won't be anything like that!" said Mrs. Bean.

"Tain't likely, Mrs. B.," said her husband. He looked after Leslie, who had hurried away without explaining. "Tryin' to be funny, I expect, the smart aleck—by cracky," he said. "I bet that's where the name came from."

"What name, Mr. B.?"

"Smart aleck. Short for 'smart alligator!' " And he made the fizzing sound behind his whiskers that was the only way you could tell when he was laughing.

But the ducks, Alice and Emma, who were sitting between Freddy and Jinx, the black cat, began looking around nervously. "Oh, sister," said Emma, "I do wish we'd taken dear Uncle Wesley's advice and stayed home. If there's a panic—"

"Dear me," said Alice. "I should think it might be interesting. I've never been at a panic."

Jinx looked around and grinned at them. "There's no call to be upset, girls," he said. "Panics are lots of fun. My old dad used to take us kittens to every panic that was held within a radius of ten miles. I guess he'd still be attending 'em if he hadn't tried to attend two in one evening. Kind of overestimated his staying power."

"How dreadful!" said Alice. "What happened to him, Jinx?"

"Trampled and squashed. But he was a good father while he lasted."

"He's kidding you, Emma," said Freddy. "There won't be any panic." But to himself he said, "I wonder if Mr. Boom's dilemma is mixed up with a panic somehow? Golly, a dilemma and a panic—that's too much for even Mr. Boom to handle!"

But there wasn't any sign of either for a while. The show started and the acts followed one another smoothly, and the clowns came tumbling out, and one of them—a kangaroo with a perpetually scared look painted on his face—kept Mr. Bean fizzing like a leaky soda water bottle. For when anybody called him, or touched him on the shoulder, he would jump. Only he didn't give just a little jump; he went ten feet in the air. Mr. Bean pointed his pipe stem at him. "That one there, Mrs. B.," he said—"He kills me." And he fizzed some more.

But Mrs. Bean didn't think he was funny at all. "That jumping jack?" she said. "I don't see anything to laugh at in him." Her black eyes twinkled. "Why you yourself are twice as funny. I get more fun out of watching you trying to keep awake in church than out of all such hopping around."

Pretty soon Mademoiselle Rose came out and did some trick riding on Dexter. She danced and stood on her head and jumped through hoops and the audience applauded and shouted until the tent walls shook. They would have applauded just as loud if she had ridden around the ring without doing any tricks at all, she was so popular. Mademoiselle Rose knew this, and so she had thought up some extra stunts—for like all performers, she wanted her skill to be appreciated. So first they brought in Jerry, the rhinoceros, and she rode him around, standing on her head; and then they brought in Rajah, the tiger.

Rajah looked up at the row upon row of peo-

ple in the audience and roared angrily, and
everybody was very still. Mademoiselle Rose
went towards him and he backed away, snarling, and everybody said: "Oh!" under their
breaths. They weren't scared of course for they
all knew Rajah; he had been with the circus
for years, and had many friends in Centerboro;
indeed when the circus was in town he got
more invitations than he could accept, for he
was a fine storyteller, a good dancer, and enter-
taining without being noisy. But he had now of
course to act as bad tempered and ferocious as
possible, so that Mademoiselle Rose would seem
to be in danger.

So he snarled and snapped, and made swipes
at her with a paw as big as a broom, and the audience shuddered and squealed, and a little girl
in the top row began to cry. Which was foolish
of her, because only that morning Rajah had
been sitting on her front porch, telling her
stories about the jungle. He had never been in
the jungle, which is probably why his stories
were so exciting. So the little girl's mother
slapped her and she stopped crying; and by that
time Mademoiselle Rose had vaulted on to
Rajah's back and he went tearing around the

ring, pretending to try to throw her off. And just then Freddy's old friend, the sheriff and a small fat man in a black suit and a derby hat shouted: "Stop the show!"

Mr. Boomschmidt rode towards them. "Here, here!" he said. "Good gracious, you can't come in here like this, upsetting things."

"Sorry, Mr. Boom," said the sheriff, "afraid I have to. It's my duty."

"Oh, it's you, Sheriff," Mr. Boomschmidt said. "I didn't see you. That is, I did see you, but I didn't know it. I mean—well, you know what I mean. Glad to see you, now that I do."

"Well, I ain't glad to be here," said the sheriff. "But they ain't given me any choice. This here—" he pointed at his companion, "is Mr. Nuisance—"

"Newsome is the name," said the little man.

"That's what I said—Nuisance," said the sheriff.

"But the name is—" the other began.

"Shut up, will you?" the sheriff snapped. "Now, Mr. Boom," he went on, "this here Nuisance is lawyer for a man named Watson P. Condiment." He stopped and said: "Condiment. Condiment. Guess I can't do anything with that

Stop the Show

name." Then he went on. "And this here Condiment, he claims that by forcin' this young lady, Mademoiselle Rose, to appear in public performances with rhinoceroses, lions, tigers and other unmanageable animals and wild and ferocious beasts of the jungle, you, the hereinafter—" He stopped again. "Or was it 'heretobefore'? Can't remember; Nuisance, where's that paper?"

Mr. Newsome handed him a folded paper, and the sheriff opened it. "Ha!" he exclaimed. "'Twasn't either one. Guess I better read it. '—you, the abovementioned Orestes Boomschmidt, are placing the aforesaid young lady in great jeopardy and danger of life and limb, and further, that by allowing the said unmanageable animals to wander about freely, unrestrained by cages, bolts, bars, muzzles or other protective measures, you, the abovementioned Orestes Boomschmidt, are endangering the life, liberty and pursuit of happiness of the residents of Centerboro. And we therefore direct the sheriff to forcibly restrain you, the aforesaid Orestes Boomschmidt, and to compel you to cease, desist and refrain from the abovementioned practices, and if you refuse we direct the sheriff to place you under arrest pending investigation.'

"There," said the sheriff. "That's said real pretty, but it don't mean much."

"It's very nice, Sheriff," said Mr. Boomschmidt, who apparently hadn't understood what it was all about. "I like hearing you read aloud. Is there any more?"

"Isn't that enough?" demanded Mr. Newsome. "You heard what the sheriff said. If you don't want to go to jail, you have to take Mademoiselle Rose out of the show."

"Take me out of the show? Nonsense!" said Rose. She stood beside Rajah, with one hand resting on his shoulder. She looked very pretty.

"My goodness gracious!" said Mr. Boomschmidt, "Rajah, are you unmag, unmalla—oh, well—a wild and ferocious beast of the jungle? I never should have suspected it, never! I shall have to keep an eye on you, I guess." He walked to the edge of the ring and faced the audience. "My good friends," he said, "this gentleman is a Mr. Nuisance. He wants the sheriff to arrest me, because he claims that Rajah here, is dangerous. Says he eats two or three little boys every day for breakfast—"

"I never said—" Mr. Newsome began angrily.

But the sheriff said: "Shut up, you! Go on, Boom."

"Well, my gracious, if Rajah does things like that, I want to know about it," Mr. Boomschmidt went on. "I know that Rajah has been around town all morning. And I'll just ask you— have any of you missed any of your little boys today? Have you even heard of any that are missing—or any dogs or cats—"

"Hey, boss," said Rajah reproachfully. "Be reasonable!"

"Dear me, of course, Rajah; excuse me. I know you wouldn't eat anybody's pets. Well, friends, what do you say? Shall we lock Rajah up and do the show without him?"

The audience stood up and shouted. "No, no; we want Rajah." "Throw Nuisance out and go on with the show." And two men in the front row threw pop bottles at Mr. Newsome. One of them zipped past the ear of the kangaroo clown, who was so startled that he forgot to jump.

"Well, well, that settles that," said Mr. Boomschmidt. "Now, Mr. Nuisance—"

"I keep telling you," said the little man angrily, "that the name is *Newsome*."

"Newsome—Nuisance; what's the differ-ence," said Mr. Boomschmidt. "It's what a man *is* that counts. Eh, Leo? Isn't that so?"

"Right, chief," said the lion, who had joined the group in the ring. "Want I should chew his arm off?"

"Later, Leo; later," said Mr. Boomschmidt. "Now, sheriff, if you'll clear the ring—"

"Sorry, Mr. Boom," said the sheriff, "but I've got my duty to do. I've got to investigate this case before the show can go on. This claim that Rajah is dangerous—"

"Me dangerous?" said the tiger. "You kid-ding, sheriff?"

Mademoiselle Rose said: "I know you don't want to stop the show, sheriff. Tell us what you want us to do, and we'll do it."

"Well, ma'am, this tiger has been called dangerous. You got to prove to me that he ain't."

"Why that ought to be easy," said Mr. Boom-schmidt. "Why he's so gentle a baby could ride him."

"Oh, indeed!" said Mr. Newsome sarcasti-cally. "Well, I wouldn't want my baby to ride him."

"I wouldn't want him to either," said Rajah, "if he takes after you."

Mr. Boomschmidt addressed the audience again. "Ladies and gentlemen, you have heard what Mr. Ah—this man says. To prove how gentle Rajah is, we now offer free rides around the ring on his back to any boy or girl—my gracious, yes—any man or woman who wants one. You have Rajah's personal guarantee that no harm will come to them."

There was a buzz of conversation along the benches, but no one came forward. Several wives poked their husbands hopefully and said: "Go on, Henry, what you afraid of?" and a number of husbands tried to persuade their wives that a ride on a tiger would be fun. But nobody volunteered.

"Golly," Freddy said to Jinx, "somebody's got to start this, or Mr. Boom won't be able to prove his point." And he got up and vaulted over the barrier into the ring.

Mr. Boomschmidt shook hands with him and thanked him, and Rajah grinned and licked his chops. "If I was hungry, Freddy," he said, "I can't think of anybody I'd rather invite to breakfast than you."

"All right, tiger," Freddy said. "No fancy stunts, now. And none of your jungle jokes. Remember, I'm not Mademoiselle Rose."

"It would be hard to forget it," Rajah said. "Though I don't know," he added, "put a little ballet skirt on you, and you'd look real cute."

So Freddy got on Rajah's back and they started around the ring at a long easy lope. Freddy was a little nervous at first. He had his own horse and was a fine rider, but he had never ridden a tiger before. As a matter of fact it was very comfortable. When he dismounted at the end of the ride the audience, led by Mr. Bean, gave him three cheers; and then a number of other people volunteered for a ride. The last one, before the show went on again was the little girl who had started to cry when Rajah first came in.

At this the sheriff expressed himself as completely satisfied that Rajah was no more dangerous than a kitten. Mr. Newsome protested of course, but the sheriff hustled him out, and Mademoiselle Rose went on with her act.

For some time afterwards Mr. Bean kept fizzing and slapping his knee, and at last Mrs. Bean turned to him and said: "Land of liberty, Mr. B., what *are* you giggling about?"

"That man," said Mr. Bean. "Nuisance, the sheriff called him. That was good, that was!"

"Fiddlesticks!" said Mrs. Bean. "I don't see that was so smart. Easy enough to make up that kind of a joke on somebody's name."

"Fiddlesticks yourself!" he replied. "You couldn't make up anything on our name—Bean."

"Pshaw, that's easy," she said. "I could call you—" But he never found out what she could call him, for at that moment two chariots came rumbling into the big tent and lined up for the start of the chariot race.

"Cracky!" said Mr. Bean. "Look at that second chariot!"

CHAPTER

3

When the Bean animals arrived at the circus,
Mr. and Mrs. Bean and the smaller animals
were shown to front row seats. But Hank, and
the three cows, Mrs. Wiggins, Mrs. Wurzburger
and Mrs. Wogus, were too big to sit on the

benches, so Mr. Boomschmidt let them stand right down in the ring, beside the doorway where the performers came into the tent.

Just before Mademoiselle Rose started her trick riding, Bill Wonks came out and talked to Mr. Boomschmidt for a minute; then he came over and said to Hank: "We're getting ready for the Roman chariot race, and the boss thinks maybe you can help us." And when Hank said sure, he'd do what he could, Bill explained. "There's been three white horses on one chariot, and three black horses on the other. But Mr. Huber, the middle horse on the white team, has got the hiccups. 'Twouldn't matter with a smaller animal, but horse hiccups are pretty big hiccups, and I guess it would look pretty silly to have a horse hiccupin' in a chariot race. The boss thought maybe you'd take his place."

"Well, I dunno," said Hank slowly. "I'd like to accommodate Mr. Boom, sure enough. But I ain't as young as I was, and I got the rheumatism in my off hind leg something fierce. Makes me yell when I take a quick step. Guess a yeller would be sillier than a hiccuper. Though I dunno; maybe not. Hiccupin's pretty silly."

"Take me," said Mrs. Wurzburger suddenly. "I'm mostly white, and if you harness me between the others, nobody'll notice."

Bill shook his head. "You couldn't keep up. Those horses run fast."

"So do I," said the cow. "I won the two-twenty free-for-all at the Tushville Fair last fall, and there were two horses in it and a boy who's on the track team at Hamilton College." And as Bill still shook his head, she said, "All right, I'll prove it. I'll race you out to the gate and back."

Bill grinned. "O K," he said, "if you beat me you run in the chariot race."

Most cows are slow and clumsy runners, but now and then you find one that is a real racer, and Mrs. Wurzburger was one of these. "I have to be known for *something*," she used to say. "Sister Wiggins is proud of being known as Freddy's partner in the detective business. And Sister Wogus—well, being dumb isn't usually anything to be proud of, but she's so dumb that —gracious, you can't believe it. It's a gift. But I wasn't famous for anything. 'She's that middle one,' they used to say. So I took up track work." And indeed she was wonderful over hurdles.

So Hank said: "Ready, get set, go!" and they

started. They were about even when they reached the gate, but Bill Wonks wasn't in training, while Mrs. Wurzburger always kept herself in pretty good shape and dieted and went to bed early. So after they turned back, Bill began to fall behind. There wasn't anybody around outside except the ostrich, who was selling tickets, and a couple of elephants whose job was to walk around the tent and pull out any little boys who were trying to crawl in under the canvas without paying admission. But when the elephants saw a cow running, with Bill in pursuit, they thought that Mrs. Wurzburger had crashed the gate, and that Bill was chasing her to make her pay up.

"Hey, you; stop! Where you going?" they yelled, and started to head her off. And then Mrs. Wurzburger did something which won her undying fame. One of the elephants was directly in her path. But she didn't stop. She just put on a burst of speed and leaped. She leaped right over that elephant, and went on into the tent.

So Bill came panting up and explained to the elephants, and then he went in and, without saying a word, harnessed Mrs. Wurzburger be-

She leaped right over that elephant.

tween the two white horses and the two-wheeled chariots rumbled into the ring.

It was always hard to surprise Mr. Boomschmidt because he had seen a lot of queer things in his time, and also because he was one of those happy people who find almost everything queer and interesting. He blinked when he saw the cow between the two horses, and then he just climbed into their chariot, and gathered up the reins, and Bill got into the black chariot.

They were to race three times around the ring. The two white horses were pretty scornful of the cow. They laughed right in her face and said they were ashamed of being seen in such company. But they would have done better to keep still, for once the race started, Mrs. Wurzburger tore along at such a swift pace that she practically dragged them around the ring.

But the race never finished. Just as they were starting around on the second lap, with the two chariots rattling and thumping along side by side and the audience all standing up and waving and yelling, there came from high up in the air outside the tent the whine of a diving plane. The sound increased suddenly and terrifyingly to an almost deafening whistling roar; and there was great confusion in the audience, some people jumping up to try to escape and others diving under the benches. The two men pulled their chariots to a stop, and Mr. Boomschmidt jumped out and began shouting to the terrified audience. But of course nobody could hear him.

Then as suddenly as it had come the sound diminished.

But the show had been spoiled. The people had been thoroughly frightened, and their only thought was to get out as quickly as they could. They scrambled for the exits, falling over one another in their anxiety to get away; and Mr. Boomschmidt, who had stopped trying to calm them, called to Bill to tell Oscar to give all the people their money back.

Alice and Emma had been pretty scared when the plane had buzzed the tent. Emma had put her head under her wing and trembled. Alice however was made of sterner stuff. She trembled a little too, but then she looked at Mr. Bean to see how he was taking it, and when she saw him puffing away peacefully on his pipe and not even looking up at the tent roof, she stopped trembling and nudged Emma with her wing. "Sister!" she whispered. "Take your head out and stop that shaking! What would Uncle Wesley say!"

"I know what old Wes would do," said Jinx. "He'd tremble so that he'd loosen half his tail feathers."

The sisters knew it too, but they always pretended that their pompous little uncle was a sort of mixture of George Washington and Wild Bill Hickok. Dignified but dashing; the bravest of the brave. "You wouldn't dare say that to his face!" Alice said, and Emma pulled her head out to say: "I guess you wouldn't."

Mr. Bean turned to look up at the rapidly emptying benches behind him. "Well, Mrs. B.," he said, "guess that concludes the show." He got up and walked down to speak to Mr. Boomschmidt. "Congratulations," he said. "Fine show. Specially that there last act with the airplane. Fine way to get your audience out quick as soon as the show is over. Don't see how you ever thought of it."

Mr. Boomschmidt said: "I didn't. That isn't our plane. Good gracious, we try hard to scare our audiences. That's what a lot of 'em come for —to be scared by ferocious wild animals. But we

don't want to scare 'em right out of the tent—so
bad we have to give 'em their money back."

"Didn't scare me," said Mr. Bean. "Didn't
scare Mrs. B. either. Thought it was part of the
show."

"My goodness gracious me," said Mr. Boomschmidt. "That gives me an idea! Maybe we
could advertise it as part of the show. Gracious,
it really is part of the show anyway. Even though
I don't know whose plane it is. It has followed
us all the way up from the South. Does that dive
on the tent in the middle of every show. Then
everybody runs and I have to give their money
back. Another month of it and the show will
have to fold up."

"Well who is it—whose plane is it?" Freddy
asked.

But Mr. Boomschmidt paid no attention.
"New added feature," he said. "That's the way
we'll advertise it. Never before presented by
this or any other circus. Thrilling sensation! Be
dived at by bomber! Oh golly, what an idea! Eh,
Leo, isn't that a wonderful idea?"

" 'Twon't work, chief," said the lion. "Can't
be done."

"Oh, *Leo!*" said Mr. Boomschmidt disgustedly. "What is the matter with you? Why do you always have to throw cold water on my ideas?"

"Because you'll be in hot water if I don't," Leo said. "Ha, not bad, eh? No; look, chief, suppose you advertise it and the guy comes and drops some of those dummy bombs full of flour on the audience the way he did in Altoona last week. Or suppose you advertise it and he doesn't show up at all?"

"We must be gettin' along, Mrs. B.," Mr. Bean said. He looked at Mr. Boomschmidt. "Dilemma," he said, and then turned and pointed his pipe stem at Freddy. "Better let him tackle it." Then he turned and led the animals out of the tent.

"Well, Freddy; Mr. Bean's right," said Mr. Boomschmidt. "That's my dilemma. Do you suppose you can help me?"

Freddy didn't answer at once. He put on his Great Detective expression. He stuck out his chest and pulled in his chin and looked down his long nose at Mr. Boomschmidt. "I have no doubt we can solve this case, which does not seem to offer much difficulty. Whom do you suspect?"

Mr. Boomschmidt looked puzzled. "Whom?"

he inquired vaguely. Then he said: "Oh, I see. Well, good gracious, whom do we suspect of what?"

"Why, of annoying you, of course," Freddy said. "Of trying to put the show out of business."

"Oh," said Mr. Boomschmidt again. "Good gracious, we don't suspect anybody, do we Leo? Because we don't know who's doing it. So how would we know who to suspect—I mean 'whom,' " he added.

"Oh, come on, chief," said Leo. "Quit kidding around. Tell him about old Condiment."

Mr. Boomschmidt could talk straight and to the point when he wanted to. Usually he didn't want to. He pretended to be a lot more simpleminded than he was so as to mix people up— which was fun for him. It was also useful, for if someone came to him with an objection or a complaint, he could mix them up so thoroughly that usually they forgot what they wanted to say. Indeed, often they turned right around and disagreed with themselves.

So now he laughed and said: "Well, well, Leo, perhaps you're right. You see, Freddy, this Mr. Watson P. Condiment wants to marry our

Rose." And he told how Mr. Condiment had tried to buy the circus and how mad he had got when he was informed it wasn't for sale. "He wants to put the circus out of business," Mr. Boomschmidt said, "and my goodness, what better way is there to do it than to drop bombs on it?"

"H'm," said Freddy importantly. "Ha. I see." He thought for a minute, then said: "I gather, then, that you think the airplane belongs to Mr. Condiment?"

"Oh, we're sure of it, aren't we, Leo? But we can't prove it. We complained to the police in several towns, and they checked up on all private planes, and watched, but they can't find out whose plane this is or where it comes from. We figure he must have a secret landing field somewhere. If you could only find it—"

"We'll find it," said Freddy. "Just leave everything to us, Mr. Boom. You have nothing further to worry about."

Freddy called this sort of talk "building up your client's confidence in you." It didn't mean that he had any plan or knew what to do, it just meant that he wanted Mr. Boomschmidt to think that he did. Of course it didn't fool Mr.

Boomschmidt any. But he knew Freddy pretty well, and he felt sure that the pig was smart enough to think up something.

So he said: "Why, Freddy, that's fine. I can't tell you how happy I am that you're going to take this case.—Now, why do I say that? Why shouldn't I be able to tell you? Leo, do you know any reason why I can't?"

"Sure, chief," said the lion. "Maybe you don't think he's smart enough to solve it."

Freddy didn't bother to answer him. He walked off to consult his partner, Mrs. Wiggins.

CHAPTER
4

Mrs. Wiggins was talking with Mademoiselle Rose, and when Freddy came up she turned to him. "My land, Freddy," she said. "I can't do a thing with this girl. You talk to her, will you?"

"What's the matter?" he asked.

Rose smiled at him. "Why I was just telling your partner here, Freddy, that I can't let things go on like this. I can't let Mr. Boom's business be ruined on account of me."

"You mean you'd marry that old Condiment?" Freddy exclaimed.

"What else can I do?" she said. "Even if you found some way of getting rid of the airplane, he'd think of something else. Like today, trying to prove that our animals are dangerous. That wouldn't work in Centerboro, but it does in places where we've never given a show before. No Freddy, I've decided—there just isn't any other way."

"Mr. Boom thinks there is," Mrs. Wiggins said. "That's why he came straight to Centerboro. Freddy is going to think up something."

"Eh?" said Freddy, and then he said hastily: "Oh, sure, sure. I've got half a dozen ideas—just want to decide which is the best one. Yes, sir; before Frederick & Wiggins get through with that old Condiment, he'll . . ."

Rose interrupted him. "Look, Freddy, I know you want to help and maybe in time you really would figure out some plan. But we haven't got any time. Every time that plane buzzes the tent and drives the people out, it costs Mr. Boom a lot of money. He'll go broke before you can do anything. I know you've been successful in some pretty tough cases, but this is one where I'm afraid you can't do anything till it's too late. I'm the only one that can save Mr. Boom, and I'm not going to put it off any longer."

"Well, good land," said Mrs. Wiggins, "you ought at least to give Freddy a chance to tell you what his plan is." And she looked confidently at her partner.

It is nice to be admired, all right, but it is sometimes kind of embarrassing. That was one trouble with Mrs. Wiggins. She was always so sure that Freddy knew just what he was doing that she never hesitated to ask him—usually in front of people. And since, like most detectives, he trusted more to luck than to planning, he had to make up something quick. Right now with them both looking at him expectantly, he put on his most confident smile. Behind it of course his mind was a complete blank. "Ah," he said significantly. "To be sure. Yes, yes, of course." And then an idea did pop into his head. Without looking at it very closely he brought

it out. "I'm going to find that secret air strip,"
he said. "I'm going to get a plane and chase that
fellow, next time he comes over."

"Gracious!" said Mrs. Wiggins, and Rose
said: "But Freddy, you don't know how to fly."

"There are a couple of instructors over at the
flying field," he said. "Jimmy Witherspoon has
been taking lessons. They let him solo after he
had had just eight hours of instruction. I'm just
as smart as Jimmy."

"Smarter," said Mrs. Wiggins loyally. "But,
land of love, Freddy—not smart enough to go
tearing around the sky after somebody that
might shoot at you."

"Anyway, there's not time," said Mademoiselle Rose. "If that plane spoils three or four
more performances, Mr. Boom will have to
close down."

"He won't give any more performances until
I can fly," said Freddy. "Look here. Suppose he
stays in Centerboro and gives everybody a
month's vacation, puts off the next show until
I'm ready to go up and chase that plane away.
Will you wait that long? I just know we can
manage if we have a little time."

"Well. . . ." said Rose doubtfully. "I think

it's crazy, Freddy. But . . . yes, I'll go talk to Mr. Boom. If he O K's your scheme, I'll wait too. But after that, if you haven't any results to show—well, I'm just going to say yes to Mr. Condiment."

"All right," Freddy said. "Mrs. Wiggins, you get all the information you can about this Condiment. I'm going over to the airfield."

Freddy was in luck. One of the instructors, Johnny Guild, hadn't had any pupils for ten days and he snapped Freddy up. "We don't usually take animals," he said. "But I don't know why not. It'll be a great feather in my cap if I have taught a pig to fly." He looked sharply at Freddy. "You *are* a pig, aren't you?"

"Why, sure," said Freddy, "what else would I be?"

"Oh, nothing, I guess. Only . . . well, you look so much like my Uncle Rollo. Still, I suppose it's only a superficial resemblance. Hope so for your sake. Made him seasick to ride a bicycle." He grinned. "Well, come on." And he led Freddy over to the trainer plane and had him get in and began explaining the instruments and controls.

Freddy learned quickly, and Johnny had so

much free time that he was able to give him several hours a day. Freddy had expected to be scared, but he wasn't, even when he made his first solo flight. On the third flight he made alone he flew over the Bean farm. It was funny to look down and see the farm spread out below him like a map, the barnyard surrounded by all the buildings, and his own little house just above it, and then beyond, the other farms— Macy's and Witherspoon's and Schermerhorn's. And then beyond them again—looking no distance at all from the air—the towns that were some of them half a day's journey away—Tushville and Centerboro and South Pharisee—and far to the west some little toy building blocks that were Syracuse.

He and Johnny got to be good friends, and after a time he told Johnny about Mademoiselle Rose and Mr. Condiment and why he was learning to fly. Johnny was pretty doubtful about the scheme. "I saw that plane that came over and buzzed your circus," he said. "I think it's an old army plane from the last war. That means it cruises at 300 miles an hour anyway. It can fly rings around any plane that you or your Mr. Bean could probably afford to buy."

"Mr. Bean isn't going to buy any plane," Freddy said.

Johnny laughed. "Maybe I hadn't ought to tell you," he said. "But Mr. Bean was out here the other day. He was watching you practising loops and rolls. He stood there puffing so hard on his pipe I thought he'd set those whiskers afire. He kept saying: 'Is that Freddy? Is that my pig?' as if he couldn't believe it. And then he began asking me how much planes cost. And— well, he ended up by making a down payment on one that Ed Platt brought here to try to sell. It's a Sky Cruiser and has been flown less than a hundred hours. It's not as simple as this trainer, though in some ways it's easier to fly."

"Oh golly!" said Freddy. "Where is it? Can I see it?"

"You ought to wait till Mr. Bean shows it to you. Stay home tomorrow; I think he's asked Ed to fly it out to the farm."

Freddy didn't say anything to the other animals about what Johnny had told him, so that when Ed Platt set down the plane in the upper pasture next morning they all rushed up from the barnyard, supposing that it had perhaps been forced down by engine trouble. Sniffy Wilson caused a slight panic among some of the younger animals by shouting that it was a space ship. "The Martians have landed!" he yelled. "Run! Hide! These are terrible creatures from another planet!"

Some of the rabbits and one or two field mice ran off and hid, and Uncle Wesley started immediately for the woods.

He tried to persuade Alice and Emma to go with him, but they knew that Sniffy got most of his ideas from the comics he was always reading, and that there wasn't likely to be much sense in anything he said; so they didn't go. Uncle Wesley didn't come back for nearly a week and he only reappeared then because he couldn't find anything to eat in the woods and he decided that there was less chance of being cooked and eaten by Martians than of starving to death if he stayed where he was.

Ed Platt climbed out of the plane and shook hands with Mr. Bean and the animals stood around in a circle and watched. The two men talked a minute, and then Mr. Bean turned and crooked a finger at Freddy. So Freddy went forward.

Mr. Bean looked at Freddy, then he looked

at the plane. He cleared his throat several times, and at last reached out and laid his hand on the wing. "Yours," he said. "Your plane." And then as if feeling that perhaps something more in the way of a speech of presentation was needed, he said, "Good pig. Good pilot. Only pig pilot in the country. Frederick Bean. Proud of ye." He gave Freddy a whack on the back and turned and stumped off towards the barn.

The animals all cheered. They cheered for Mr. Bean and they cheered for Freddy and then they cheered for the plane. But a stranger, a muskrat named Lyman, who had stopped in to call on Sniffy Wilson, snorted contemptuously and said to Jinx: "Grumpy old codger, ain't he? Acts like he hated the pig." And he criticized Mr. Bean for several minutes.

"Look, friend," said Jinx finally. "Mr. Bean isn't a yap-and-jabber man like some folks that drop in here from time to time. When he says, 'Good pig,' it's the same as if he made a long speech and hung a medal on Freddy and fired a salute. If he looks at you and nods, it's the same as if I put my paws on your shoulders and kissed you on both cheeks. Like this," he said and sprang at the muskrat.

"Hey, quit" said Lyman. "I didn't mean anything. I—"

"O K, then; beat it," said Jinx. And as the rat hesitated: "I might get feeling affectionate towards you again, any minute." So Lyman went.

"Well, Freddy," Ed Platt said, "there she is. She's a nice ship. Lucky you've got this level field, though it's a little short, Mr. Bean is going to take down that fence—throw these two fields together. Then you'll have a pretty fair air strip. Well suppose I take you up and show you how she works."

So they went up and Ed put the plane through its paces, and then they came down and changed places and Freddy took it up.

"You did fine," Ed said when they had landed again. "But you shouldn't take her up alone for a day or two. She handles easier than the trainer, but she's a lot faster and there are more chances to get into trouble. I'll come out again tomorrow."

Mr. Boomschmidt agreed to Freddy's plan, although he wasn't very hopeful about it. But he said a vacation would be good for his animals. Of course they had had what was practically a vacation all winter long, but Mr. Boomschmidt said that his father had always told him that you couldn't have too much of a good thing. So the circus stayed in camp at the Centerboro fair grounds, but there wasn't any performance, and the animals could do what they pleased all day long. They had lots of friends in town, and these people invited them to dinner and to play cards, and it was altogether quite a gay season. Indeed they were simply deluged with invitations. Even Hannibal, the elephant, dined out nearly every evening, and it is no joke ordering dinner when you have an elephant as guest. Not when you have to provide a ton or two of hay. Jerry, the rhinoceros, was the only one that didn't get many invitations. Everybody liked him, but he didn't see very well and was always breaking dishes or sitting down in chairs that weren't strong enough for a rhinoceros. And he was not a very good card player either. Old Mrs. Peppercorn felt so sorry for Jerry though, that she gave a lawn party for him, and it was quite a success. Jerry was so happy when he said goodbye he cried, and he leaned against a corner of the porch and the whole porch collapsed with him. Then he cried harder than ever, but Mrs. Peppercorn said he mustn't feel

The whole porch collapsed with him.

bad, because she only rented the house and so the porch wasn't really hers anyway. So Jerry felt better.

In the days while Freddy was learning to fly, nothing was seen of the mysterious plane. Evidently Mr. Condiment, or whoever owned it, had some way of finding out that no performances were to be held. Mrs. Wiggins sent Rabbit No. 23, one of the firm's best investigators, around to question various people, but he learned little of interest. Mr. Condiment's lawyer had left town again after his failure to have Mr. Boomschmidt arrested, and Mr. Condiment himself was presumed to be at his home in Philadelphia, where he had some sort of a publishing business. Mr. Boomschmidt said that he probably would show up in Centerboro soon; because he hadn't proposed to Mademoiselle Rose since they left Altoona, and he'd been coming and begging her to marry him about once a week ever since early spring.

Of course there had been a good deal of talk about Freddy's flying lessons, and within a week or so stories of the flying pig had got into the papers, and several reporters had come up from New York to interview him. There had been

a big story about him in the *Times* magazine
section, with pictures. And the result of all this
publicity was a telegram from Mr. Bean's Uncle
Ben, who was now living in Chicago, announc-
ing that he was coming to spend a few months,
to do some experimental work in his old shop
in the barn loft, in which work he needed the
assistance of an experienced airplane pilot.

CHAPTER

5

Mr. Benjamin Bean was an inventor. While at the farm on a previous visit he had invented a number of useful gadgets—a cake of soap which would not slip out of your hand in the bathtub, an alarm clock which shot off a series of firecrackers, and most important of all, a clockwork

boy named Bertram who could do almost anything a real boy could when he was wound up
and operated by some animal small enough to
get into the little control room between his
shoulders.

Uncle Ben was a nice person to have around,
for if anything got broken or out of order, he
could fix it as good as new. Sometimes even better than new. For when he had fixed an article,
it often seemed to have turned into something
entirely different. Like the time Mrs. Bean's
washing machine broke down, and he fixed it,
and afterwards it wouldn't wash any more, and
when you turned it on it got very hot, so they
used it as an oven to keep Mr. Bean's supper
warm when he was late. But Uncle Ben was
even less of a talker than Mr. Bean. So when he
came rattling through the gate a couple of days
later in an old station wagon, and climbed out
and shook hands with the Beans and with all the
animals without saying a word, nobody was surprised. "You're just as much of a chatterbox as
you always were, Uncle Ben," Mrs. Bean said,
and he grinned and patted her on the shoulder.
Then he pointed to the station wagon which
seemed to be full of tools and pieces of machin-

ery. "Shop," he said. So the animals pitched in and carried everything up the narrow barn stairs into the old shop.

Everything but a square black box, which had knobs on one side and a sort of eyepiece on top, which he lifted out himself and set on the porch. Lettered on the side in white letters were the words, "The Benjamin Bean Bombsight. Pat. Applied For."

"So that's what you've invented!" said Mrs. Bean. "And you want Freddy to experiment with it, I suppose? Well, you're not going to drop any bombs on this farm, and you can make up your mind to that right now!"

"Dummies," said Uncle Ben. "Go 'pop' not 'boom.' "

"I don't care if they go fizzle-wizzle-wizzle," said Mrs. Bean firmly. "I won't have them around."

"Now, Mrs. B.," said Mr. Bean, "don't fly off the handle. Uncle Ben's never blown us up yet. Though I won't say he ain't tried. Remember that mouse trap that had the blank cartridge in it?—didn't kill the mice but supposed to scare 'em so they'd run off and never come back. We set a dozen that night, I recollect. Then about midnight—cracky, it sounded like they'd opened fire on Fort Sumter!"

Mrs. Bean laughed but she still looked dubious. "Those traps were ten times as noisy as they needed to be," she said. "And I'll wager these bombs will be, dummies or not. Never knew a Bean yet, man or boy, that didn't want to make as much noise as possible."

Freddy didn't know whether he was pleased or not that Uncle Ben had come. Experimenting with the bombsight might be fun, but it would take time, and he was going to be pretty busy trying to trace down that mystery plane. On the other hand, Uncle Ben was a fine mechanic, and now he wouldn't have to go down to Centerboro every time he wanted anything on the plane checked.

Freddy was never an early riser, and when he got up next morning and went up to the pasture to see if everything was all right, he found that Uncle Ben had been there working on the plane for several hours. The Benjamin Bean Bombsight was installed, and he was working on the release for the bombs. Freddy wasn't very well pleased. It was his plane and he didn't think anybody should start making changes in it without his permission. But he knew that Uncle Ben was too good a mechanic to do anything that would hurt the plane or slow it down in flight; and he thought that if the bombsight worked well, maybe he could use it. Anyway, it would be fun to try it out.

When Uncle Ben had finished, he showed Freddy how to work the bombsight. As you flew along, you looked in the eyepiece, and saw the fields and houses you were flying over pass under you. There were two white lines in the glass, and when your target came opposite where these lines crossed, you pressed the release and dropped your bomb. According to Uncle Ben, you hit the target right on the nose every time. Indeed, he was so sure of this that he had already arranged for a delegation of army officers to fly up to the Bean farm that day and he was going to put on a test for them. He showed Freddy a telegram from a General Grimm, stating that he and various other members of the armed forces would arrive at two o'clock sharp.

"Gracious!" said Freddy. "That isn't much time to practise!"

Uncle Ben smiled. "Foolproof," he said.

"Maybe it is," said Freddy. "But maybe it isn't pig-proof."

So they picked a big rock in the middle of the pasture as a target, and Freddy went up. He made two or three practise passes over the field. Looking in the bombsight he could see the rock plainly, and Uncle Ben standing way up by the stone wall that bounded the pasture on the north. It wasn't easy to steer the plane so that the target appeared in the right place in the glass, but at last he got it and pressed the bomb release.

Freddy didn't see what happened for he was banking to swing around and drop another bomb. But some of the animals who had come up to find out what was going on, saw it. The bomb was a very small dummy one, and when it was released, it came whizzing down, but instead of whizzing towards the target, it whizzed straight at Uncle Ben. Uncle Ben jumped the wall and fell flat on his face behind it just as the bomb hit the wall and went pop! If it had been a real bomb, neither Uncle Ben nor that section of wall would ever have been seen again.

The animals all ran out and picked Uncle

Uncle Ben jumped the wall and fell flat on his face.

Ben up and dusted him off, and just then Freddy made another run and dropped a second bomb. And as that came whizzing down Uncle Ben and all the animals threw themselves flat behind the wall. And pop! went that bomb within a foot of where the other one had hit.

Freddy saw then that something was wrong and he brought the plane down. Uncle Ben stood shaking his head sadly as the animals related what had happened. "Bad," he said. "Bombsight useless."

"Why, no it isn't," Freddy said. "It just doesn't hit where you aim it. Now if we put up a flag on the wall here and call that the target, and then I go up and aim at the big rock, I'll hit the target every time."

Freddy would have liked to try once or twice more, but by this time it was nearly one, and Uncle Ben was already late for dinner, and of course after dinner would have to wash his hands and put a necktie on to welcome General Grimm. So Freddy fixed the target flag on the stone wall, and left two rabbits to guard the plane, and went to get his own dinner.

Exactly at two o'clock two large planes landed in the pasture and out stepped two generals,

five colonels, and twelve other officers of as-
sorted ranks. General Grimm was short, stocky
and red-faced and looked as if his uniform was
too tight for him but nobody had better mention it. He led his companions over to where
Uncle Ben was standing beside Freddy's plane.
"Benjamin Bean?" he shouted.

"Me," said Uncle Ben, holding out his hand.

General Grimm shook it. "Pleased!" he
roared.

"Same," said Uncle Ben.

The general glared at him for a moment. He
was famous throughout the whole army for saying as few words as possible in as loud a voice as
possible, and he wasn't very pleased to find
someone who used even fewer words, even
though in a quiet voice. He waved a hand at
the other officers and named them. "Major General Grumby, Colonel Queeck, Colonel Tablet,
Colonel Drosky," and so on.

Uncle Ben bowed to each, and then indicated
Freddy, who was standing beside the plane.
"Frederick," he said. "Pilot."

Freddy bowed. In a crash helmet and goggles
he didn't look like a pig. He might have been
just a short and rather too plump young man

with a long nose. Then he climbed into the plane and Uncle Ben swung the propeller.

The flag had been put on the wall where the two bombs had fallen, and Uncle Ben pointed to it. "Target," he said, and General Grimm nodded, and his face relaxed, for he had gained a word on Uncle Ben. But Freddy was worried. As he taxied down to the end of the field for his take-off, he wondered if he hadn't better just forget about the bombsight and use his own eyes to decide when to drop the bomb. For General Grimm was standing right on the rock now, to get a clear view of the flag, and grouped about the rock were Uncle Ben and the officers. "Suppose I aim at the rock this time," Freddy thought, "and instead of hitting the flag, the old bombsight works right and the bomb hits the General. Golly, I suppose they'd just shoot me!"

However the only thing to do was to aim at the rock. After all, he had done that both times before, and the bombs had hit right smack where the flag was. Indeed he needn't have worried. He dropped his two bombs and one of them actually knocked the flag off the wall.

General Grimm went up to shake hands with

him as he climbed out of the plane. "Fine!" roared the general. "Excellent!" Then he turned to Uncle Ben. "Army needs your bombsight," he shouted.

"Thanks," said Uncle Ben, and the general glowered at him again, for Uncle Ben had gained three words at one clip.

Then as soon as the other officers saw that General Grimm liked the bombsight, they all began to praise it to the skies, and to say that Uncle Ben had better begin making more of them right away, because the Army and the Air Force would have to put one on every bomber. But the other general, Grumby, went and whispered to General Grimm, and after a minute he said to Uncle Ben: "The Benjamin Bean Bombsight appears to be just what the army has been waiting for. But of course we will have to test it out more thoroughly. I would like to try it myself, and with your permission I will go up and drop a couple of bombs on the target myself."

"Delighted," said Uncle Ben. He had evidently forgotten that the bombsight now hit about a hundred and fifty yards to one side of where it was aimed. He went and picked up the two dummy bombs that Freddy had dropped, and put in the things that went pop! when they hit the ground, and attached them under the wings. Freddy didn't dare say anything. He watched as General Grumby climbed into the cockpit, and he groaned as General Grumby taxied off for the take-off.

General Grumby was a little insignificant looking man, but he was a magnificent flier. When he had gained altitude he tried out the plane—did loops and side slips and rolls—and then he went on up until he was almost out of sight. They could see him going over the field, then banking to come around and pass over it again. But they didn't know when he dropped the bombs. At least they didn't know when he dropped one of them. But the other—well, the first Freddy knew about it was when there was a sort of rushing, whistling sound, and all the officers yelled and fell flat on their faces. And then there was a loud pop! and Uncle Ben said "Wow!" and Freddy said: "Oh my gracious, goodness me!" For the dummy had come down and hit within two inches of General Grimm's left ear, where he was lying on the grass. And it had gone pop! right in his face, which was all black on one side.

Of course all the officers jumped up and helped the general to his feet, and brushed him off, and asked if he was hurt. He didn't know the side of his face was black, and I guess they knew better than to tell him, because he was mad enough anyway.

"You're witnesses!" he shouted. "I'll have Grumby court-martialed for this! Deliberate attempt at murder!"

"No harm done," said Uncle Ben. "New man, Grumby. Not expert with Benjamin Bean Bombsight. Like to see another test?"

It was clever of Uncle Ben, Freddy thought, to use more words than the General had. And indeed the realization that he was now ahead in the word-saving contest, seemed to calm General Grimm. But he shook his head. "Test next week," he said. "Without Grumby." He turned to his staff. "Prepare to take off," he shouted.

"I think," said one of the colonels, "that the general feels that, in view of this unfortunate occurrence, it would be better to make another test at a later date. He will write you in a day or two. He is, I think, much pleased with your bombsight, and—" He broke off, for up the slope from the barnyard came Mr. Bean with a shotgun in the crook of his arm.

"What in tarnation's going on up here?" he demanded. "Uncle Ben, what you done—declared war on your family?"

"War?" said Uncle Ben.

Mr. Bean said: "That's what it seemed like when that little pop-bomb of yours hit the corner of the porch. Scared Jinx into a fit. Scared me, too."

General Grumby had brought the plane down, and Mr. Bean watched him climb out. "What's he doing in your plane, Freddy?" he asked.

Freddy explained. "But," he said, "I don't know exactly why the bomb dropped down by the house."

"Exactly?" said Mr. Bean. "H'm, you don't know exactly?"

"No, sir," said Freddy, "not *exactly*."

Mr. Bean looked at him sharply. Evidently he understood that the pig didn't want to make any further explanation in front of the officers. He turned to General Grimm. "Well, sir," he began, but the General was glaring and shaking his fist at General Grumby, who was walking towards him. "Murderer!" shouted General Grimm.

"Oh, come, Grimm," said General Grumby. "If I wanted to murder you, I wouldn't take a plane up and drop bombs on you. Too expensive."

"Scoundrel!" roared General Grimm and shook his fist.

But General Grumby put his arm around General Grimm's shoulders and shook him gently. "You'd better go wash your face," he said, "and I give you my word, Grimm—you too, Mr. Bean—that I wasn't playing any tricks. Frankly I don't understand what happened. I aimed at the flag, both times—had it right under the crosslines. The bombsight must be defective."

"No!" said Uncle Ben.

Freddy realized that the only thing to do was to gain time. If he told how he had had to aim way to one side of the target in order to hit it, the army wouldn't have any further interest in such an unreliable weapon. "You saw me hit the target with both bombs," he said. "I can do it fifty times more, if that will convince you. But I think as General Grimm has suggested, it will be better to set another day for another test."

General Grimm hadn't suggested any such thing, but he wanted to get away from General Grumby, who was kidding him about having fallen on his face to escape from a bomb that just went pop. "Next week," he said. "Same day, same hour." Then he turned to Mr. Bean. "Regret damage," he said. "Send bill to Washington—Department of the Army."

"Oh well, guess I won't bother," Mr. Bean said. "Busted a small hole in the porch floor, but that'll be handy to knock my pipe ashes into. Scared the cat—lemme see; to shock and mental anguish caused in cat, resulting in loss of one or possibly two lives—oh, say, ten cents. No, guess I won't bother. I'll make it up to Jinx with cream tonight."

"Good afternoon, sir," shouted General Grimm. "Let me alone, Grumby," he said, shaking off his friend, and stalked over to his plane.

CHAPTER

6

After General Grimm and his officers had gone, Uncle Ben took the bombsight down to the shop, and went to work to fix it so the bombs would hit what they were aimed at. And then Freddy got in the plane and flew down to Centerboro.

First he went to see Mr. Boomschmidt. "Could you start giving shows again tomorrow?" he asked. "I think I can fly well enough now to do something about that plane if he tries to break up the show. At least, I can get an idea where he comes from."

"Comes from different directions," said Mr. Boomschmidt, "but when he goes, he nearly always goes north. —Oh, my goodness, I almost forgot—Mr. Condiment is in town. Called on Rose last evening. He's staying at the hotel."

"I must have a look at him," Freddy said. "Maybe I can figure out a way to get rid of him."

"Oh please, no rough stuff!" said Mr. Boomschmidt anxiously. "He'd really have proof then that our animals were unmang—unmanj—oh, my gracious, you say it, Leo."

"Unmanageable animals, chief," said the lion.

"I don't see how you do it, Leo," said Mr. Boomschmidt admiringly. "Goodness, I can say 'The black bug bled on the bare barn floor,' and 'She sells seashells,' and all those tongue twisters, but this unmang—unmaggabubble . . . no, I can't do it."

"Well, don't cry about it, chief," said Leo.

"There's a lot of things you can do that I can't do."

"Dear me, such as what?" Mr. Boomschmidt asked.

"Why, standing on your head, for one. Remember, last Tuesday at Mr. Beller's party you did it, and after we got home I tried it, and I've been trying ever since, but I just can't get my hind legs up."

"Really, Leo?" said Mr. Boomschmidt. "Now that's very interesting. Now look." He took off his plug hat and put it on the ground and then stood on his head. "See, Leo? Now if you just flip over quick . . ."

Freddy went back to his plane. He owned a great many different costumes which he used as disguises in his detective work, and he had decided to keep a couple in the plane, just so that if an important case came up he could hop into a disguise and take the trail before it got cold. He had a new disguise which had been given him by an old and rather dressy friend, Mrs. Winfield Church, and he thought he'd try it. It was a thin dress with big flowers on it, and high-heeled shoes, and a very broad-brimmed picture hat, with a veil. It was a sort of garden party outfit.

Freddy tapped along up Main Street in his high-heeled shoes, and a number of people turned to look at him, for he made really a very fashionable figure. Mr. Watt, the optician, standing at the door of his shop, said: "Some class, hey?" to Miss Peebles (Harriet—Hats; Latest Paris Creations); and Miss Peebles said: "Yes, indeed, a very fashionable turnout. I wonder who she is?"

Freddy went into the hotel, and the clerk bowed so low that he hit his nose on the counter. Then he sneezed and in answer to Freddy's question said no, Mr. Condiment had gone out.

So Freddy went to look for him. He stopped in front of the Busy Bee Department Store and asked a sparrow who was sitting on the awning if he'd seen a thin, sour-faced stranger anywhere in town. The sparrow, who like most sparrows was always trying to be tough without much to do it with, said out of the corner of his beak: "Yeh, I seen the guy you want. He went in old Tweedle's bookstore." Then he slouched along the awning until he could see under the picture hat. "Boy oh boy!" he said. "If it isn't our Freddy! Well, ain't you the sweetie pie!" And he began to yell to the other sparrows to come look.

Freddy didn't want to attract attention, so he hurried off to the bookstore. He had spent a great many hours in this store, and had bought a lot of books there. Mr. Tweedle was an old friend. He was rather a peculiar person. He never even looked up when a customer came into the store, and anybody that wanted to could stay there all day taking down books from the shelves and reading them. "I used to have a bell on the door," he told Freddy, "but so many smart-alecky boys kept sticking their heads in and shouting: 'Hey, Tweedledum, where's Tweedledee!' or some equally brilliant remark —well, I took it down." The funny thing about him was that although everybody in town called him "old Mr. Tweedle," he really wasn't old at all, and didn't look old. He explained that to Freddy. "Men that keep old bookstores are supposed to have long white beards and be covered with dust, just as college professors are supposed to be so absent-minded that they ought to be locked up, and army sergeants are supposed to be rough, tough men with jaws like flatirons. As a matter of fact most of these people aren't like that at all. Why, if you'll excuse me, Freddy —take pigs. They're supposed to be stubborn, and dirty and lazy. But I don't know any that are like that. Just the opposite, in fact."

When Freddy entered the store, Mr. Tweedle was having an argument with a thin, sour-faced man. "My dear sir," he was saying. "I don't sell comics. You're wasting your time."

The other sniffed. "You're wasting yours, running this kind of business. Bet you don't get two customers a week. Put in a line of Condiment Comics and from the minute you open in the morning the place'll be jammed, teeming, populous—I mean to say, crowded." He pulled a sheaf of bright-colored comic books out of his pocket. "Brighten up the place," he said.

"Look," said Mr. Tweedle; "I consider the comics cheap and silly, and I'm not going to sell my customers cheap and silly stuff."

"Half the people in the country read them," said Mr. Condiment.

"Then half the people in the country ought to go back and start all over again in the second grade," said Mr. Tweedle.

Freddy gave what he considered a ladylike cough, and when they turned to look at him he came forward and said in a high affected voice with what he fancied to be a Spanish accent: "Oh, those delightful comicals! I see you have new ones. I may look, no?"

Mr. Tweedle shrugged and turned and went into the back of the store. But Mr. Condiment squeezed his face into what was meant to be a smile, and said: "Of course, madam. Delighted, I'm sure; charmed, very happy—in short, greatly pleased. These—I publish them myself; you see my name here: Watson P. Condiment—these are the funny ones, Chirpy Cheebles, about a bird, you see—very amusing. And these are the horrible ones: Lorna, the Leopard Woman, In the Lair of the Great Serpent, The Secret of Grisly Gulch—all very grim, ghastly, shocking— in short, revolting."

"How lovely!" said Freddy, taking them. "The Great Serpent—Ah, *si!* Is he not cute? He just goes to bite that little boy in two. Oh, and see thees demon woman! Is living in Grisly Gulch, no? Oh, oh, see—she has horns! And *two* little boys she is eating!"

It was lucky that Freddy had on a veil, for he had noticed something in the back of the store and he couldn't keep his face straight—it kept spreading into a broad grin. For what he had noticed was Willy, the boa constrictor from the circus, curled up in an armchair by Mr. Tweedle's desk. At least he was partly in the chair, which wasn't large enough to hold all of him; four or five feet trailed off on the floor.

Willy was a rather unusual snake, for he was fond of reading. Snakes don't usually care much about books, probably because they haven't any hands to hold them with. But Mr. Tweedle had a sort of reading stand on his desk, and if he propped a book up on it, Willy could turn the leaves with his nose. He had spent many happy hours here when the circus was in town. He was particularly fond of poetry. That too is rather unusual in a snake.

Freddy turned a page. "Ay, *mi alma!*" he exclaimed, and then speaking in a good loud voice: "What a so dreadful creature! Indeed, how terrible to see a great serpent like that rear up beside you!" He held out the picture and then began to peer fearfully under counters and into dark corners. "Ah, Señor, think what might lurk in such darknesses! Then the springings out! The grabbings!"

Willy had lifted his head and turned to look at them. His forked tongue began to flicker out. He hadn't recognized Freddy, but he dearly loved a practical joke, and now he saw a chance for a good one. He uncoiled and flowed out of the chair, glided silently along the wall—and suddenly reared up until his big flat head with the black expressionless eyes was about an inch from Mr. Condiment's.

"No cause for alarm, ma'am," Mr. Condiment was saying. "Such creatures never really existed. They are imaginary, fictional—in short . . ." Then he saw Willy.

For a second he didn't say anything or do anything, but he had rather lank, colorless hair, and Freddy said afterwards that it rose right straight up on his head.

And then Willy said: "Hello. Want a little hug?"

This was Willy's standard greeting. But Mr. Condiment didn't know that. He gave a yell that made everybody outside on Main Street look around and say: "I wonder where the fire

Willy said: "Hello . . . Want a little hug?"

is?" and then he left, and I guess it was lucky the door was open or he would have taken it right with him.

"Thanks, Willy," said Freddy, and the snake turned sharply and stared at him.

"Freddy?" he said. "Well, for Pete's sake!" And he began to laugh so hard that he shook all the way down to the end of his tail. "My, my, aren't you pretty! I bet you drive all the boys crazy. Golly, I've just got to hug you, Freddy."

It was Willy's idea of a joke always to pretend to be so glad to see his friends that he had to hug them, and then he'd throw a couple loops around them and squeeze them until their eyes stuck out.

"Don't stop me now," said Freddy. "That's old Condiment, and I have to talk to him. I've got an idea. I think maybe I can scare him into letting Rose and Mr. Boom alone."

So Willy said all right, and he could have a rain check on the hug.

Mr. Condiment had made straight for the hotel, and Freddy caught up with him in the lobby, where he had dropped into a chair and was mopping his forehead.

"Oh, Señor Condimento, is wrong something?" Freddy asked. "You feeling sick?"

"Sick!" Mr. Condiment exclaimed. "That dreadful snake!"

"Snake?" said Freddy. "Why, Señor, I no see snakes. We just look at picture of snake in those comicals."

"This was no picture," Mr. Condiment said. "Why, it was right between us!" He stared at Freddy. "You mean you didn't really see it?"

Freddy gave a little tittering laugh. "Why, Señor Condimento!" he said. "You trying to frighten me?"

He stared at the pig, "You really didn't see anything?"

"You know what I think?" Freddy said. "Me, I just little Spanish girl, I got no brains much. What I think—that comical, Lair of Great Serpent. You make that book, you see it many times. Well, you just dream it. Awake-dreaming, yes?"

"I don't know," said Mr. Condiment dismally. "That was a dreadful experience, a horrible occurrence—I mean to say, a ghastly happening."

"But it hoppen only once, is no bad. Oh *si*, if all comicals come alive—Lorna, the Leopard Woman, Demon Woman of Gristly Gulch—"

"Grisly," said Mr. Condiment.

"*Si*, gristly. Be bad, no?"

"Don't," said Mr. Condiment, covering his eyes with his hand.

"*Bueno,* I not say more. Because—oh, Señor, I see you in these bookstore; I say to myself: is kind, that *hombre*, has kind face. He no be mad if I ask him advice."

Nobody had ever told Mr. Condiment that he had a kind face before, and even he himself probably knew that it was a pretty poor description. But the funny thing was that when he took his hand down and looked at Freddy, there really was an almost kind expression in his eyes. "Glad to do what I can," he said. "Anything within reason—in short, any assistance that is purely verbal."

"Ah, Señor!" Freddy was getting tired of the 'Señor' but it certainly sounded good and Spanish. "Lorna is not clever, but Lorna know if man and woman is kind and good. My mother say to me: 'Lorna,' she say, 'maybe you talk foolish, and no can get out of fourth grade in school, but one thing, you will be able to pick good husband.' You married, Señor Condimento?"

"I am affianced," he replied. "Betrothed—that is, engaged."

"Ay di mi!" said Freddy. "Is my bad luck!"

Mr. Condiment was looking at him suspiciously. "What did you say your name was—Lorna?" he demanded. "What's your last name?"

"Del Pardo," said Freddy. "Lorna Del Pardo is silly name, no? Condimento so much prettier. Lorna Del Condimento—so distinguished sounding. Could break these engagement, Señor Condimento?"

"Del Pardo!" said Mr. Condiment. It was the last name of Lorna, the Leopard Woman in his comic books. He looked scared, and he got up quickly. Without another word he walked out of the room.

Freddy went over to the desk, behind which Mr. Ollie Groper, the proprietor, was sitting. Mr. Groper heaved himself to his feet. "Good afternoon, madam," he said. "If you require a temporary local domicile, this hostelry is prepared to offer accommodation suitable to your requirements, however exigent."

"What lovely language!" said Freddy with a giggle. Then he lifted his veil and said: "I wish I had time to swap polysyllables with you, Mr. Groper, but I've got a lot to do and I need your help."

"Freddy!" Mr. Groper exclaimed. "Well now ain't this an unanticipated gratification! And these modish habiliments! Well, well; command me, duchess," and he shook with laughter.

So Freddy told him about Mr. Boomschmidt's dilemma, and how Mr. Condiment, by making the circus go broke, was trying to force Mademoiselle Rose to marry him. "He's got Mr. Boom over a barrel," he said, "and unless I can do something soon, Rose will just have to marry him. I'm trying to do something about that plane, but I'm trying also to scare old Condiment off. I'm trying to work the same scheme on him that he is working on Rose. Now here's the idea."

Mr. Groper laughed so hard while Freddy was telling him that he had to be helped into his chair. But he agreed to do everything that Freddy wanted. "This here Condiment ain't nothing but a human streptococcus and if I can hasten his departure from this hostelry—" The rest of his speech was rather long, and Freddy did not understand it very well, though he gathered that Mr. Condiment did nothing but complain about everything in the hotel, which he appeared to blame for his stomach ache.

"Tomorrow evening then," Freddy said as he left.

"Tomorrow evening," Mr. Groper agreed. "I anticipate a pretty gol-darned diverting *soirée.*"

CHAPTER

7

Freddy always admitted frankly that he was lazy. And yet the more he had to do, the more he seemed to accomplish. He explained it this way: He said that when a lazy person once really gets started doing things, it's easier to keep on than it is to stop. He said it was as much of an effort to stop working and sit down as it was to get up and start working in the first place. But whatever the reason was, he certainly got through a lot of work the day after the bomb-sight trial.

The first thing he did, he got up—and that, he felt, was always something of an accomplishment. For according to his theory of laziness, when you're *in* bed it's a great effort to get *out*. Just as when you're up and doing things, even when it's past bedtime, it takes a lot of persuasion to get you to go *to* bed. Freddy claimed that laziness was the only thing that could explain it. "It's the same bed," he said. "Why should you hate to get into it at night when you're going to hate to get out of it next morning?"

While Freddy was having breakfast, he thought about dilemmas and quandaries, and then he got a paper and pencil and wrote out several advertisements.

*Are you puzzled? Are you per-
    plexed?*
Try our friendly Dilemma Serv-
    ice.
No charge for consultation.
FREDERICK & WIGGINS,
Bean Farm, Centerboro 24, N. Y.

There was of course no postal zone 24 in Centerboro; Freddy just put that in to make it
sound important.

Another advertisement read like this:

*Have you a Quandary in your
    home?*
Well don't just sit there, chewing
    your fingernails.
Send for Frederick & Wiggins, the
    Quandary Specialists.
We remove quandaries and di-
    lemmas quietly, and without
    fuss.
    (Also predicaments.)

After breakfast he sat down and wrote a short
poem for the next issue of the Bean Home
News. It was another in the series of poems
which he called "The Features," and it went
like this:

THE HAIR

The hair is an adornment
  Which grows upon the head;
It's black or yellow, brown or grey,
  Occasionally red;
      But never blue or green or puce;
      Such colors would look like the deuce.

That's just one pig's opinion—
  Some have a preference
For hair that's not so usual,
  For colors more intense.
      They go for violet or carmine,
      And think that pink is simply charmin'.

So if you're really anxious
  To change to green or red,
Just tell your barber what you want
  And when he soaps your head,
      The functionary who shampoos you
      Will tint your hair light blue or fuchsia.

Aside from being pretty
  The hair can be of help
If someone bangs you on the head
  So hard it makes you yelp;
        If you have hair that's thick and tangled
        You're not so likely to get mangled.

Without hair you'd look funny,
  And rather like a squash,
And every morning you would have
  A lot more face to wash.
        Your face would go up past your fore-
            head,
        And you'll agree that would look horrid.

Grass only grows in summer,
  Hair grows the whole year through;
It must be mowed quite frequently,
  And raked twice daily, too.
        Your hair (called "locks," and some-
            times "tresses")
        If never combed, an awful mess is.

Yet some folks never cut it—
  Prefer to let it grow.

This has advantages of course,
* And even though it's slow,*
*   In time they get enough to fill a*
*   Small mattress, or to stuff a pillow.*

Having no hair himself, Freddy soon ran out
of ideas about that commodity, and he laid the
poem aside and went up into the shop where
Uncle Ben was hard at work. But he wasn't
working on the bombsight, which had been
shoved under the bench. He was making a very
complicated drawing of what looked like a
rocket. Sitting on a stool beside him were Sniffy
Wilson and Mrs. Wilson, and several of the
little Wilsons were stretched out on the floor,
looking at comics.

Uncle Ben glanced at Freddy and nodded.
"Jet plane," he said, pointing to his drawing.

"But what's become of the bombsight?"
Freddy asked.

"Bombsight's all right," Uncle Ben repeated.
"Sell it to the enemy."

Freddy thought a minute, then he laughed.
"I see," he said. "If we have a war, then you sell
the bombsight to our enemies, and their bomb-
ers won't be able to hit any of their targets. Not

a bad idea. But how about General Grimm's visit next week?"

Sniffy said: "We've been talking about that. Uncle Ben will tell General Grimm that the bombsight can't hit anything it's aimed at, but he'll persuade the General to make a good report on it. Then Uncle Ben will go see some enemy spy and sell the bombsight to him. The enemy will probably rely on General Grimm's report, and won't even try out the bombsight, but will go ahead and manufacture them and put 'em on their planes."

"Lots of 'if's' and 'maybe's' in that scheme," Freddy said. "But I suppose it might work. How about this jet plane? Isn't it pretty expensive to make?"

Sniffy said that Uncle Ben planned to pay the cost with the money he would get from the enemy spy for the bombsight. "I really gave him the idea for it," he said proudly. "I mean, he had been working on it before, but I got him to take it up again. You see, the kids and I were taking all our old comic books down to Lyman —you know, he's the muskrat that lives in the swamp, down below the flats—and Uncle Ben wanted to see them. In one of them . . . Aroma" he said to his wife, "let's have that one you're looking at."

Freddy glanced through it. It was the story of a trip to the moon in a space ship. "Uncle Ben seemed interested in this," Sniffy went on. "And I said: 'Why don't you build one yourself?' So he dug out these old jet plans and went to work on 'em. He'll build this first, and he says if he can make it do a thousand miles an hour, then may be next year he can build a bigger one to go to the moon."

"Oh, pooh!" said Freddy disgustedly. "You and your old comics! You must really believe all the foolishness in them. But I thought Uncle Ben had better sense."

Uncle Ben glanced around. He didn't say anything. He winked at Freddy and then went back to his drawing.

"Well, you see, Freddy," Sniffy said, "maybe you're right about the comics. That Robin Hood book you lent me—golly, that's some book! Why, all those adventures and things, they might have happened. Oh, the comics are kind of fun, but you know nothing like that ever really happened. Well anyway, I used to exchange comics with Lyman, but I never liked to let him take any I wanted to keep, because he lives down in that old swamp and he gets 'em wet, and then when he brings 'em back they're all mildewed."

"They look kind of mildewed to me," said Freddy, "even when they're dry."

"They do, don't they?" said Sniffy. "Spotty, like. I guess they don't have very good artists to draw the pictures. Not like in books. Anyhow, I thought if you'd lend me your other books to read, I might as well let Lyman have all these comics, because we wouldn't want 'em any more."

Freddy heard a scuffling sound behind him, then several sharp clicks, and somebody said: "Ouch!" He swung around to see that two of the little skunks had squared off and were whacking at each other with sticks. These sticks were about as long as the skunks were, and half an inch thick; they held them by the middle and tried to rap each other with each end alternately.

"Quarterstaff," said Sniffy. "We got it out of the Robin Hood book. We're going to have some bows too, and arrows. Uncle Ben is going to make them for us."

Freddy went over and pulled the bombsight out from under the bench. He picked it up and started with it over to a table. He was looking in the eyepiece when he walked across the floor, and then suddenly he stopped, backed up, went forward, backed up again—

"Hey, Freddy, what's the matter with you?" Sniffy demanded. "You taken up ballet dancing or something?"

"That's funny," Freddy said. "Look here, Uncle Ben. See that nickel on the floor? Somebody dropped it, I suppose. Well, every time I carry the bombsight over that nickel, there's a little flicker of light in the eyepiece."

Uncle Ben didn't say anything, but he dropped his pencil and took the bombsight from Freddy. He walked back and forth over the nickel, looking in the eyepiece; then he put some other coins on the floor, and some small pieces of iron and brass, and walked back and forth over them. Then he set the bombsight on the bench and grinned triumphantly.

"Well, for Pete's sake," said Sniffy. "What's it all about?"

He was looking into the eyepiece when he walked across the floor.

Uncle Ben still didn't say anything. He dipped a brush in a can of black paint and painted out the words "Benjamin Bean Bombsight. Pat. Applied For," and then he dipped another brush in a can of white paint and painted in the words "Benjamin Bean Money Finder. Pat. Pending." He looked at that for a minute, and then he took a chisel and cut a slit in the top of the bombsight large enough to take a quarter. After which he painted out the words again, and lettered in: "Benjamin Bean Improved Self-filling Piggy Bank. All Rights Reserved." He smiled happily. "Sell millions," he said.

"Well, in the first place, it doesn't look like a piggy bank," Freddy said crossly. Being a pig himself, he had never much liked the idea of piggy banks. "And in the second place," he went on, "instead of making a lot of them and selling them, and having everyone picking up lost dimes and quarters, why not just keep this one for yourself? Then all the lost dimes and quarters would be yours."

Uncle Ben shook his head. "Henry Ford," he said. "Not just one car."

"You mean Mr. Ford would have been selfish

if he'd just made one car and driven around in
it himself?"

"I guess it would have been better if he had,"
Sniffy said. "All these millions of cars, running
all over the country every which way, and
bumping into each other. Know how many of
our people are killed every year by cars?"

Skunks are rather conservative animals. That
is to say, they don't care much about new inven-
tions. They have never really approved of the
automobile, and that probably is why so many
of them get run over. They just don't like cars,
and they won't get out of the way.

Uncle Ben picked up the bombsight—which
had now become the improved piggy bank—
and held it out to Freddy. "Try it," he said.
"Garden."

"I haven't got much time," Freddy said.
"The circus is giving a performance this afternoon, and I have to be there, to see if I can find
out where that plane that keeps buzzing the big
tent comes from. But come on, Sniffy; we'll take
a whirl around the garden."

Nearly every plot of ground that has been a
garden for many years is full of things that peo-

ple that have been working in it have dropped
—coins and pencils and jackknives and all sorts
of odds and ends. After a rain is the best time to
look for them, because then the dirt will be
washed off them and they are easier to see. And
you'd be surprised how many valuable things
are sometimes found—gold rings and diamond
stickpins and brooches with pictures of Niagara
Falls enameled on them and such things. Mr.
Bean had once found a glass eye in his garden,
although there was no record of any one-eyed
man ever having lived in the neighborhood
since Revolutionary times.

Freddy and Sniffy spent about an hour in the
Bean garden, and in that time they found thirty-
seven cents, four empty brass cartridge cases,
an old-fashioned gold watch (the works were
rusted out but the case was still bright), two
brass buttons off a Civil War uniform; and Mrs.
Bean's silver spectacles that she had lost one day
ten years ago when she was picking potato bugs.

It was fun going over the garden with the
Benjamin Bean Self-filling Piggy Bank, but
Freddy had to get down to Centerboro. He left
Sniffy hunting for more coins and got Mrs. Wig-

gins to go up in the pasture with him and swing the propeller so he could start the engine of his plane. Then he flew down to the Centerboro Fair Grounds, and about half-past two, when the audience had all gone into the big tent, he took off again. He climbed to 5000 feet and then cruised slowly in a circle, watching the northern sky.

Even when he was learning to fly, Freddy had never been scared. He had always been afraid of heights, too. You couldn't have coaxed him up on the barn roof for a hundred dollars. But now, looking down through a mile of empty air on the little white oval that was the big tent, he wasn't the least bit nervous. The empty blue sky, and the two or three little cream puff clouds so dazzling white in the sunshine, made him want to sing. There was nobody there to stop him, so he did.

"Oh, the young pigs fly
　About the sky
　　And they zoom and dive and roll;
　They yell and whoop
　As they spin and loop
　　Under the sky's blue bowl.

They sing and shout
As they whiz about,
  For there's elbow room in the sky;
And it's lots more fun
Up there in the sun
  Than down in their stuffy sty.

Oh, the pig is bold
And when he's told
  That a hurricane's on the way,
Does he turn and run?
He does like fun!
  He hollers and shouts Hurray!

Oh, not a fig
Cares the fearless pig
  When the thunder bangs and crashes;
Right into the heart
Of the storm he darts,
  And plays tag with the lightning flashes."

Freddy stopped singing for a minute. That
was kind of a dark cloud rolling up over the
western horizon. Maybe a thunderstorm, he
thought; maybe he'd better beat it for home.

But in a minute the cloud thinned and vanished, and he went on singing.

"Oh, wild and free
Is a pig like me!
   When the moon is riding high
I dive and swoop at her,
Whiz around Jupiter—
   Oh this is the life for I!"

All at once he stopped singing. The northern sky wasn't empty any more. Right in the middle of it there was a tiny black dot, which grew larger and larger. It was another plane, coming in at a low altitude.

Freddy kept between the newcomer and the sun, so as not to be spotted. The plane came on fast, circled once, and then slid down in a shallow dive towards the big tent. It pulled out of the dive so close to the tent that it almost seemed to have touched it, then climbed and banked, and as the panic-stricken people came pouring out of the exits, it dove again and dropped what looked to Freddy like bombs. There were three of them, and when they hit the ground among the running people, they seemed to explode in a big puff of white smoke.

"Sacks of flour," Freddy thought. "That's what Mr. Boom said he dropped. I suppose they come down slow so they're easy to dodge and don't hurt anybody, but they scare 'em and spoil their clothes. My, that's a mean trick!"

When the flour sacks had been dropped, the plane headed north. Freddy kept well above it and followed. He felt pretty sure he hadn't been seen. Below him fields gave way to the blue water of Otesaraga Lake, and then the dark green of foliage as he flew over the lower fringe of the Adirondack forest. But he was dropping behind. He watched the plane as long as he could see it. He checked the direction with his compass, then when it finally disappeared, turned back.

Mr. Boomschmidt was pretty unhappy. "We had three hundred and eighty-six paid admissions, Freddy," he said. "But we gave four hundred and sixteen people their money back. That's what happens every time, and my gracious, I don't see why. How can more people come out of the tent than go into it? Leo has some explanation—you tell him, Leo; perhaps he can understand it; I can't."

"Oh gosh, chief, have I got to go over that again?" protested the lion.

"You don't need to for me," Freddy said. "I suppose some of the people come to the gate and ask for their money back twice. It isn't very honest, but I guess there are some people around town that would do it."

Mr. Boomschmidt looked unhappier than ever. "Oh, I can't believe that," he said.

Leo looked at Freddy. "There you are," he said. "You can't ever make the chief believe that anybody would cheat him. He wants to think everybody is as honest as he is."

It embarrassed Mr. Boomschmidt to be praised, and he blushed deeply. "I'm not honest at all," he said. "I mean, I'm not any honester than you are, Leo, and I'll thank you not to accuse me of it."

"Well, dye my hair!" said Leo. "Are you calling me dishonest?" He spoke angrily, but he winked at Freddy.

"Good gracious, no!" said Mr. Boomschmidt. "Why, I'd trust you with my last cent, and you know it, Leo. Why, I'll do it right now." He fumbled in his pocket. "Dear me, I only have three cents. Now which would be the last one? I could give each one of us one—because I trust you too, Freddy. Would that—"

"Look, Mr. Boom," Freddy interrupted. "Pretty soon you won't have one last cent if we don't do something about Mr. Condiment. I'm checking on the plane; I lost him today fifty or sixty miles north of here, but he was traveling north-northeast; tomorrow I'll wait for him on that line beyond where I lost him. I'll find him in a few days. But in the meantime I've worked out another scheme and I need your help."

CHAPTER

Mademoiselle Rose and her mother, Madame Delphine (whose real name was Annie Carraway), lived in a trailer which, when they traveled, was hooked on behind Mr. Boomschmidt's big car. Madame Delphine didn't like the new trailer as well as the wagon in which she had crossed the country a dozen times; she said it wasn't homey. But the wagon had finally fallen to pieces; and now in the trailer with her she still had the armchairs with tidies on the back, and the picture of two little girls playing a duet, and all her other treasures. So she really was very happy.

In the trailer that evening the two women were trying to squeeze Freddy into a Spanish dancer's costume. There was a hook on one end of the waistband of the long full black skirt, and an eye on the other end, and they were pulling hard to make them meet.

"Can't you breathe out a little more, Freddy?" Madame Delphine panted.

"If I breathe out any more, I'll just collapse like a busted balloon," he whispered. He had to whisper, because there wasn't enough breath left in him to speak.

Rose said: "It won't do any good if we do hook it. He's got to be able to talk. Look, we can bridge the gap with a piece of tape and fasten it with safety pins. It won't show if we drape his shawl over it."

They got him fixed finally. He tried a few

experimental dance steps in the high-heeled shoes, stuffed out with paper so they wouldn't fall off. Then he went up to the mirror. "I ought to have a veil," he said.

"A Spanish dancer in a veil?" Rose said. "Tip that flat hat over one eye," she said. "And here— here's a rose. You carry that between your teeth, and nobody can tell you're a pig." She giggled. "Ah, Señorita, how be-yootiful you are!"

"Ah, *gracias,* Señorita," said Freddy. "You like to give me leetle kees, no?"

"Come on, Freddy," said Madame Delphine. "You've got to get out of here. You don't want Mr. Condiment to find you with Rose."

Freddy went towards the door. "Suppose he doesn't come tonight?"

"If he doesn't," Rose said, "I promise I'll send for him."

But Mr. Condiment came, and proposed again to Rose, and again Rose said no. A refusal always made him cross, but tonight when he left he was crosser than usual, perhaps because his stomach ache was worse than usual. And then, of course, being cross made his stomach ache harder, which in turn made him crosser. He really growled at Rose. "Very well," he said.

"Very well! You'll rue this, you'll regret it—I mean, you'll be sorry. Another week or so and your old Boomschmidt won't have a penny left to pay your salary with. And you and your mother will starve. Ha! Will you like to watch your mother grow thinner and thinner—"

"Then I can get a job with another circus as a living skeleton," put in Madame Delphine.

"Pah!" said Mr. Condiment. "Madame, this is not a matter for jests, jokes, witticisms—that is, funny business. Ponder my words, consider them, contemplate them—I mean, think them over. I will be at the hotel if you change your mind." And he left the trailer.

He had just got to the gate of the fair grounds when behind him he heard something galloping on soft heavy paws, and he swung round to see a big lion bearing down on him. "Yow!" said Mr. Condiment, and dove head first into the little ticket booth.

But the lion stopped and sat down and saluted. "No cause for alarm, sir," he said. "A young lady sent me. She would like to speak to you again."

Naturally Mr. Condiment thought that it was Rose who had sent Leo. "Ah," he said;

"changed her mind, I expect." He hesitated, but when Leo stood politely aside, he started back.

But it wasn't Rose who was waiting for him. As he stepped into the lighted trailer, instead of the two women he had just left there, a short and rather plump young woman in a Spanish costume came dancing towards him, stamping her feet and clicking her castanets above her head. She wore a flat hat tipped over one eye, and from the corner of her mouth drooped a red rose. If her nose was rather too long and her eye —the only one visible—rather too small for beauty, Mr. Condiment was too surprised to take note of these matters.

"Ah, Señor Condimento!" she cried. "You are come! Now is everything good! Ah, Señor-r-r, when you leave poor Lorna yesterday —*ay de mi!* I am so desolate! But you have reconsider, no?"

Mr. Condiment was always pale so that it was impossible for him to turn paler; he therefore turned light green. "Reconsider? Wh-what?" he asked, and felt behind him for the door handle. But someone had quietly turned the key from the outside.

"Oh, Señor!" she said reproachfully. "You make the fun, eh? You laughing at little Lorna? Is not smart, Señor."

"I'm not laughing," said Mr. Condiment. "I don't know what you're talking about."

"Maybe if Lorna dance for you, you remember?" The castanets clicked, and Freddy took a few experimental steps. But the left shoe was slipping, and what was worse, one of the safety pins on the waistband had given way. "No," he said. "Lorna is angry." He stamped his foot to show how angry he was, and he felt the skirt slip. "You have tell Lorna one beeg lie! You know what hoppen to mans who lie to Lor-r-rna Del Pardo?" He rolled the r's ferociously.

"I haven't quibbled, prevaricated, perjured —that is, lied to you," Mr. Condiment protested. "I don't even know you."

"Aha! You write books about Lorna, no?"

"Why, I—I didn't write those books about Lorna, the Leopard Woman. A Mr. Gizling writes them for me to publish. I never supposed, thought, conjectured—I mean, imagined, that there was really anyone of that name." He looked around desperately, but the door was locked, the windows closed. Luckily he did not

look very closely at the windows, or he would
have seen a sort of large moon, which was Mr.
Groper's face, looking in one of them, with a
smaller moon which was Mr. Boomschmidt, beside it.

Both moons were split by a large grin.

"Such fonny names—Señor Gizling!" Freddy
laughed bitterly. "More lies! *Si, si!* I tell you,
is no Señor Gizling. Is only Señor Condimento,
big liar! *Si*, Señor Condimento—tell me is en-
gage to marry. But Señorita Rosa, she say no, she
not promise to marry 'im." Freddy was having
a wonderful time, but the skirt was slipping
again; he decided to bring the scene quickly to
a close. His voice had a tendency to squeak when
he was pretending to be angry, so now he
dropped it to a menacing whisper. "Why so
many lies, Señor? Is that you wish to forget what
you say—Lorna Del Condimento is nice name?
Si, si, you say that—is same as ask me to marry
you."

"Nonsense," said Mr. Condiment. "I never
said anything about wedlock, nuptials—I mean,
marriage."

"No?" Freddy managed to make his voice
sound very sinister indeed. "Then maybe you

don't forget what is the revenge of Lorna the Leopard Woman, in those books your Mr. Gizling write? Ah, *si!* R-r-r-revenge!" He rolled out the word and at the same instant the lights in the trailer went out.

Mr. Condiment had backed against the door. In place of the stubby little Spanish dancer, what he saw when the light immediately came on again, was a full grown leopard, rearing up and apparently just about to fall upon him. Mr. Condiment was too scared even to yell. He made a sort of fizzing noise and fell over on his face.

"Fainted," said Freddy, coming out from behind the armchair. "That makes everything easier. Well, thanks, Harrison. You certainly looked terrifying."

The leopard grinned. "How do you think *you* look, pig?" he demanded. "I sure would rather meet myself on any dark night than you, in that rig."

Freddy dropped the rose and went towards him. "Ah, Señor 'Arrison, you like one big kees, no?"

"Get away from me," said the leopard. He walked over and looked at Mr. Condiment, then turned him over on his back with one paw.

"Ah—Señor 'Arrison, you like one big kees?"

"Silly looking fellow." He wrinkled up his nose. "I'm glad I didn't have to bite him."

Someone unlocked the door and Rose and her mother came in.

"Get behind that chair, Harrison," said Madame Delphine. She got some water and began sprinkling Mr. Condiment's face.

After a minute he opened his eyes. "Madame Delphine?" he said inquiringly, and sat up and looked around, frowning. "Where—where did you come from?"

"Come from?" she said. "I don't understand. Rose and I have been here all the time."

"But after I left, and that lion brought me back—there was a leopard—" He shuddered.

Madame Delphine raised her eyebrows and looked at Mademoiselle Rose and Mademoiselle raised *her* eyebrows and looked back. "You've been right here," said the latter. "You were about to go when you suddenly fainted. Now you've come to. There was no leopard. Only this young lady who came in a few minutes ago to see you," and she pointed to Freddy, who was sitting in the Boston rocker. He still had the rose between his teeth.

Mr. Condiment started violently at sight of

Freddy. He began to say something, but Madame Delphine said angrily: "All this talk of leopards! What are you trying to do, Mr. Condiment? You come here, forcing your attentions upon my daughter, begging her to marry you, and all the time you are engaged to this lady, Señorita Del Pardo."

"Engaged to her?" Mr. Condiment exclaimed. "Poppycock! Balderdash! That is—nonsense! Who says I am engaged to her?"

"Why, Señor-r-r!" Freddy got up, holding on to his waistband, and glided menacingly towards Mr. Condiment, who shrank back. "I say it—I, Lorna, the Leopard Woman." He lowered his voice to a whisper. "You know what happen to mans who say Lorna lie, eh? Wait—I show you." He turned and went behind the tall chair back of which Harrison was concealed, and as he disappeared, the leopard stalked out from the other side and came snarling towards Mr. Condiment. With a yell Mr. Condiment jumped up, dashed open the door, and disappeared in the darkness.

As soon as he had gone Freddy and Leo and Harrison and Mr. Boomschmidt all piled into Mr. Groper's car, and Mr. Groper drove them down to the hotel. By the time Mr. Condiment

got there, they had hidden themselves where
they could watch the desk without being seen.

Mr. Condiment came in hurriedly and went
up to the desk. He looked rather wild. He
picked up a pad of telegraph blanks and wrote
out a wire, and then banged several times on the
handbell with which the guests summoned Mr.
Groper when he was out of the office.

At that, Willy, who had been coiled behind
the counter, reared up until his head was opposite Mr. Condiment's. "Yes, sir," he said; "can
I be of assistance?"

Mr. Condiment didn't faint this time. He
made one leap to the front door, a second one to
the sidewalk, and a third one to the garage.
There was the sound of a car starting, a terrible
grinding of gears, and then the roar of the motor
died away in the distance.

They all came out and Freddy went over to
the desk and picked up the telegram, and read
it aloud.

It was to Mr. A. J. Mandible, Mgr. Condi-
ment Comics, Philadelphia, and it said: "Fire
Gizling stop destroy all copies Lorna also Great
Serpent stop fill no more orders for these books.
                    (Signed) Condiment."

"Why does he tell his manager to do something and then say: 'Stop'? Willy asked. "Funny way to run a business."

"Good gracious, that poor Mr. Mandible," said Mr. Boomschmidt. "He just starts to do something and then the boss tells him to stop."

Mr. Groper explained that owing to the impracticability of inserting proper punctuation in telegraphic communications, the word "stop," in order to obviate ambiguity, was employed as a substitute for the period. But nobody understood him.

"Well, I guess we fixed Brother Condiment's wagon for him," said Harrison.

Freddy wasn't so sure. "I guess we've made him think that the characters in his comics have come alive," he said. "I hope that's scared him enough so he won't bother Rose any more. But even if it has, he may still want to put Mr. Boom out of business."

A waitress came in and whispered to Mr. Groper, and he turned to the others. "The commisariat of this here establishment has prepared a light collation of comestibles. Kindly proceed to the prandial hall." He threw open the door of the diningroom. "Señorita?" And he offered his arm to Freddy.

CHAPTER

9

Each day for the next three days the mysterious plane came out of the north, buzzed the big tent while the performance was going on, dropped a few sacks of flour, and flew off again. Each day, a little farther north, Freddy lay in wait for him high up in the sky. And then on the third day, just before coming to the St. Law-rence River, the strange plane suddenly circled to head into the wind, and began to glide down towards the earth.

Freddy had Leo up with him that day. Most animals don't care much about flying, but the lion was enthusiastic about it, and had even be-gun to take lessons from Johnny Guild.

Leo said into his microphone: "He's landing, Freddy. Let's go right in behind him. Boy, wait till I get my paws on his neck!"

"We can't land today," Freddy said. "He's certain to have a gun. Yes, he's putting her down on that field. It's well hidden, too—trees all around it, and no houses nearby. Probably keeps the plane in that barn."

Leo still wanted to go right down and have it out with the pilot, but Freddy said no. "I don't think he's seen us," he said, "and now that we know where his field is, that gives us a big ad-vantage. We'll work out our plans tonight." And he turned back for home.

When the circus was in Centerboro, Leo often stayed all night at the farm. There was an empty box stall next to Hank's stall in the stable which served the animals as a guest room. They had entertained some very distinguished guests in that way, and Mr. Bean was never surprised when he went out to give Hank his breakfast to find a tiger or an alligator or a hyena snoring away in the box stall. So when Freddy invited Leo to stay, the lion accepted. And they were just crossing the barnyard when they stopped short. "Well, dye my hair!" Leo exclaimed.

Out of the stable came Sniffy Wilson and his wife, Aroma, followed by their seven oldest children. Each carried a long stick slanted over his shoulder, and each had a small bow and a quiver full of little arrows slung at his back.

"Hi, Freddy," said Sniffy. "I'm off to the greenwood with my merry men."

"You what?" said Freddy.

"The greenwood, the greenwood, you dope —I mean, thou knave," said Sniffy. "You ought to know, you gave me that Robin Hood book yourself."

"Oh, sure," said Freddy. He turned to Leo. "You know about Robin Hood, don't you? He and a band of outlaws lived in Sherwood Forest, in England, long ago, and they robbed the rich men that had taken their farms away from them, and helped the poor people."

"Yeah?" said Leo. "Where's Sniffy going to find any rich men to rob in the Big Woods?"

"We aren't going to rob anybody specially," said the skunk. "We're going to right wrongs. We're going to help widows and orphans."

"I'm an orphan," said Leo hopefully.

"Can you hit anything with those little arrows?" Freddy asked, and Leo said: "They aren't big enough to do any harm. Why they wouldn't stop a mouse."

Sniffy grinned at him. "Oh, is that so?" He turned to his children. "Kids—I mean, my merry men all—string your bows." And when the bows were strung and each little skunk had fitted an arrow to the string: "Now, lads," he said, "when I give the word, pin me that lion's tail to the ground."

"Hey, take it easy," Leo protested, backing off with his tail held well behind him. "I was only kidding. Why, Sniffy, you wouldn't plug an old friend with those great arrows!"

"Unstring bows!" Sniffy ordered. "No, Leo, we wouldn't want to puncture an old pal. But just in case you don't think we could . . . Violet," he said, "see that fencepost with the knot on the side? It's about fifty yards. Suppose that knot was a lion's nose, and you were hunting lions. What would you do?"

"I guess I'd do this, papa," said Violet. She was the smallest of Sniffy's children. She strung her bow again, nocked an arrow to the string, pulled back and let fly. Tock! went the arrow into the knot.

Freddy and Leo walked down to inspect it. "Well, dye my whiskers pink!" said the lion. "I'm sure glad that wasn't my nose."

"I guess it would have kind of tickled no matter where it hit you," said Freddy. "Say, Sniffy, can all your kids shoot as well as that?"

"They've only been practising a little while," said Sniffy. "Violet's the best. But the others are coming along. Matter of fact, I'm not so bad myself. Go down there by the post, Freddy, and, let's see—put that tin can on your head." He whipped an arrow out of his quiver. "Nay, pick up the can, lad. Dost thou not trust me to hit the mark?"

"You're darn right I dost not," said Freddy. "You stick the can up on the post."

"What's all this 'dost' talk?" Leo asked. "And stuff about 'merry men?'"

"It's out of the Robin Hood book," Freddy

said. "It's the way they talked in 1400 or when-
ever it was."

"I kind of like it," the lion said. "I'd like to
try it on Mr. Boom when he gets to arguing
about something."

"I'll lend you the book," said Freddy. "But,
Sniffy, if you and your merry men want to right
a wrong, why don't you help out Mr. Boomschmidt? Mademoiselle Rose is a lady in dis-
tress; don't you want to rescue her?"

"Oh, sure," said Sniffy, "I mean, aye, that we
do, Brother Pig. But I wot not how we shall be
about it."

"Well, *I* wot," said Freddy. "Come into the
stable and we'll talk it over."

Freddy had some trouble persuading the
skunks to do what he wanted them to do. His
idea was to drop them by parachute on the secret airfield at night, so they wouldn't be seen.
They could then hide in the surrounding woods
and act as spies. "We've got to find out who the
pilot of that plane is," he said, "and if there are
other men at the field. We want to know if Mr.
Condiment hires them. When you've got all the
information you can pick up, we'll be able to

plan how to attack the airfield. Then when we attack—" Freddy hesitated a minute. The Wilsons didn't look very enthusiastic. Then he remembered the talk in the Robin Hood book. "Why, how now, lads?" he said. "Ye tell me ye be bound for a life of adventure in the merry greenwood, and yet methinks ye hang back when 'tis question of trading hard knocks with a stout foe. Nay then, if your hearts be so craven, it is best that ye creep back to a safe fat life in the meadows, and leave the greenwood to those who have no fear of the sharp rap of a cudgel, or the swish of a clothyard shaft."

The Robin Hood talk, and the accusation of cowardice, brought Sniffy up to the mark. "Oh, is that so!" he said. "I mean—sayest thou so? Then out upon thee for a scurvy knave, so to miscall an old friend. We be no cravens, we Wilsons—no mice, no rabbits, to flinch from a fight. Show us what thou wouldst have us do—"

"Just a minute," interrupted a voice from the doorway. "Clear up some of this funny talk. 'Flinch from a fight'—does that mean you're calling rabbits cowards?" And Rabbit No. 18 hopped into the barn.

"Hello, 18," said Freddy. "Oh now, I don't think Sniffy meant to throw any doubt on rabbit bravery. I think—"

But Sniffy interrupted. He struck a warlike pose—probably, Freddy thought, for the benefit of his children, who were gazing at him admiringly. "If the cap fits," he said haughtily, "put it on."

"O K," said No. 18. "I'll put it on. Give me a stick, one of you kids. Now, Sniffy, on guard. You may think you're Robin Hood, but I *know* I'm the new Head Horrible of the Horrible Ten, and we'll see who's the best man."

Sniffy might well have paused at mention of the Horrible Ten. This was an association of rabbits who had banded together, partly to protect their own interests, partly to have fun going around at night and scaring people they didn't like. They pinned their big ears down and carried little tin knives, and to suddenly see these odd looking creatures dancing around you in the moonlight, flourishing their knives and chanting a bloodthirsty song, was indeed rather terrifying.

But Sniffy wasn't going to back down in front

of the children. He threw aside his bow and
quiver, and grasping his staff by the middle,
advanced upon 18.

There was a sharp little rattle as the staves
met. But the bout was a short one. No. 18 had
no skill with the quarterstaff; instead of holding
it by the middle as Sniffy did, with his paws well
apart, he seized it like a baseball bat by one end.
Then he swung. Swish! and Sniffy ducked be-
neath it. Swish—crack! Sniffy warded the second
blow with one end of his staff, then struck hard
with the other end. The blow caught 18 in the
side and knocked the wind out of him. He sat
down on the floor and said Whoosh! several
times. Then slowly he got up. "O K," he said.
"O K. So you're Robin Hood. But I'm still the
Head Horrible." And he limped out of the
barn.

"This is too bad, Sniffy," Freddy said. "Just
when we all ought to be pulling together to help
out Mr. Boom. You'll hear from the Horribles,
I bet."

"What can they do?" said Sniffy. "Look at
these arrows, Freddy. Uncle Ben made us up
some tipped with sharp wire, and a lot tipped

The blow knocked the wind out of him.

with porcupine quills. I wouldn't use the wire
ones on the Horribles. After all, most of them
are friends of mine. But if they try any of this
scary business—well, they'll have a lot of fun
pulling quills out of one another."

"I'd rather see you plugging them into Mr.
Condiment than into the Horribles," Freddy
said. "But a minute ago you said—that is, thou
saidst that thou wouldst straightway do what I
asked of thee."

"Yes," said Sniffy. "In sooth I did promise
thee that thy—" He broke off. "Golly," he said,
I sound like a teakettle—all those th's."

"I thought you were trying to whistle,"
Freddy said. "But it is pretty hard stuff to talk.
Let's quit before we get our tongues tied into
a knot. Look, there's a lot of old umbrellas up
in the Beans' attic. You can use them as parachutes—I can drop you on that airfield tomorrow night. Are you game?"

"We're game," said Sniffy. "It's for Mr. Boom
and Mademoiselle Rose. But how can we report
to you? It would take us a week to walk back."

"There's an airfield where I can land at West
Nineveh, about four miles south of where you'll
be. I'll get in touch with you in two days. When

we're over the field I'll show you where you can keep watch for me. Now let's go get the umbrellas. I think you'd better make a practise jump or two off the barn before tomorrow night."

CHAPTER
10

The Horrible Ten didn't waste much time. Freddy went and saw Mrs. Bean and she let him take the umbrellas, and then the skunks practised jumping off the barn roof with them. They worked fine. It was after dark when Freddy said they were good enough to jump from a plane. The skunks started off then to spend one last night, before leaving on their perilous mission, in their old den in the pasture. And they were just climbing over the stone wall when they heard a lot of little squeaky voices singing a sort of chant.

"Shut your eyes. Cover your head.
Or better still, get under the bed.
For the Horrible Ten are out tonight,
And they're full of meanness and rage and spite.

Oh, what is that! Does something crawl
Among the shadows along the wall?

In the dark—under the chair,
Do you see red eyes? Is there something there?

What's that reflection in the mirror?
Is it a Horrible creeping nearer?

Look! Look! Run for your lives!
I see the flash of the Horribles' knives!"

And then out from behind clumps of grass and small bushes popped the little round heads of fifteen or twenty Horribles. They came capering out and did a sort of war dance around the skunks, brandishing long sticks as well as their little tin knives, and chanting:

"Yes! Yes! We're out tonight
To giggle and dance in the pale moonlight.
Run! Run, if you'd save your skin,
For we're mean and wicked and full of sin.
We love to pinch our little sisters,
To make 'em yelp and raise large blisters;
To stick long pins in our favorite aunts;
Pour ink on our uncles' Sunday pants.
Our mothers cry and our fathers roar,
But we just run out and slam the door.
Our knives are sharp and we're close behind
*   you;*
You haven't a chance; we're sure to find you.
We're really awful; you might as well
Just lie down flat and begin to yell."

Even though Sniffy and his family knew perfectly well who the Horribles were, it was pretty scary being jumped out at by such queer looking creatures, and they bunched together for a minute and would probably have run if they hadn't been surrounded. But Sniffy yelled at them. "String bows!" he shouted. "Backs to the wall, lads. Fire at will, porky quills only. Stand fast, my merry men all."

The little skunks were well trained. In fifteen seconds the Horribles had to duck down again into their hiding places as the little arrows went whit! whit! whit! past their ears, and two of them, Nos. 17 and 12, who were slow in taking cover, let out sharp squeals as the quills stuck into them.

But the Head Horrible, No. 18, had foreseen that they would be fired on, and so had equipped his followers with sticks. "Brother Horribles," he called, "prepare to charge. Are you ready?"

"Ready! All ready, Your Dreadfulness!" came the answer.

"Then charge!" shouted No. 18. "Up and at 'em. Remember our war cry, brothers!" And the rabbits rushed out, waving their sticks, and shouting: "Charge, Brother Horribles, charge on our foes! Jump on their toes! Give them a kick and a bust in the nose! Horribles forever!"

"Spread out, lads!" Sniffy called. "Aroma, you guard the left flank; I'll take the right." He hadn't thought about a war cry, so he had to make one up quickly. "Forward, stout lads!" he shouted. "For home, for country, and for Bean! A Wilson! A Wilson!"

The Horribles hadn't intended to get into a fight. Their horribleness was really all in fun. But when two or three of them had been jabbed by the quill arrows they got mad, and a mad rabbit is a very angry animal, indeed. Rabbits are peaceful as a rule, but when roused they can be ferocious fighters, and seldom give quarter.

But Freddy had suspected that there might be trouble, and he had followed the skunks at some distance. When he heard the shrill little voices shouting their war cries, and the rattle and click of the sticks as the two parties joined battle, he hurried up to the wall and climbed over. "Hey, stop it! Quit!" he shouted. "Sniffy, get back over that wall. And you, 18, get your— Ouch!" he squealed, as Sniffy, Junior's, quarterstaff rapped him smartly on the nose. And immediately squealed again as a stick wielded by Rabbit No. 4 jabbed him in the ribs. He backed quickly out of the danger zone.

Fortunately some of the other animals had heard the row. Jinx and Robert, the collie, and Georgie, the little brown dog, came over the wall and they all waded into the fight, slapping right and left, until presently the two parties drew away from each other.

"Drop those sticks, all of you," said Robert. He was a very quiet and dignified dog who never said much, but when he took charge of things, the animals did what he told them to. The rabbits dropped their sticks at once, and then the skunks followed suit. "Now what's this all about?" Robert demanded.

"Maybe *you* can tell *me*," said Sniffy. "We were going home to bed when we were set upon by this armed band of scurvy rascals—"

"We did not set on you," said 18. "You started shooting at us—"

"You came at us with sticks," said Sniffy.

"You hit me with a stick first," 18 retorted.

"Not till you swung at me with one, in the barn," Sniffy said.

"Oh, shut up, both of you," said Jinx. "Look, Robert, you'll never find out who started it. And what's it matter? Nobody's hurt."

"Well," said Robert slowly. "Maybe. If

they'll just go home peaceably. But fighting, you know, among ourselves, here on the farm—that's one thing Mr. Bean won't stand for. If he'd heard this disturbance tonight, you know what he'd do: he'd fire every last rabbit on the place. And you, Sniffy, he'd give you and your family notice to move."

"Hey!" said Sniffy. "I never thought of that! Then we'd really be outlaws! Golly, Robert, do you suppose you could get him to do it anyway?"

Robert stared at the skunk. "Are you crazy?" he demanded.

Freddy said: "Look, Sniffy, Robin Hood was made an outlaw unjustly, by people in power who were wicked. But Mr. Bean isn't wicked, and if he outlawed you for fighting rabbits, it wouldn't be unjust. Robin Hood knew he was right, but you'd know you were wrong."

"Oh," said Sniffy. "Yes, I guess so. Anyway, if we were really outlaws we wouldn't be able to help Mr. Boom."

"Help Mr. Boom—you?" No. 18 jeered. "Golly, Brother Horribles, is that a laugh!"

"It sure is, Your Dreadfulness," replied the Horribles, and they all gave a sarcastic laugh—"Haw, haw, haw!"

This made the skunks mad again, and Petunia, Sniffy's second daughter, picked up her quarterstaff and swung at the nearest rabbit. Luckily Jinx had been watching her; he pounced and knocked the stick from her paws.

"You can haw-haw all you want to," said Sniffy angrily, "but we *are* going to help Mr. Boom, and that's more than any rabbits could do."

"Oh, is that so!" said 35.

"Yes, that's so," said Aroma. "What could a rabbit do?"

"What could a rabbit do!" 18 repeated. "Sister, are you kidding? Haven't we worked with Freddy on a dozen detective cases? Haven't we—"

"Oh, shut up! Shut up!" Freddy shouted. "We'll be yawping here all night at this rate. Look, Sniffy, I gave you the Robin Hood idea, didn't I, in the first place? And you Horribles, do you remember last year you made me a member of your society—an Honorary Horrible? All right, that gives me a right to speak for both sides here, doesn't it?"

There was some hesitation, but Jinx said, "O K, you kids; anybody that don't agree will just step aside with me for a few minutes. Yes sir, kindly old Uncle Jinx—he'll take you on his knee and pat your little heads—like this!" he yelled suddenly, and a black paw shot out like lightning and smacked a rabbit who had been furtively trying to pick up his stick.

"We agree, we agree," they said hurriedly.

"Well," said Freddy, "you most of you know that the Wilsons are going to be dropped by parachute near the field where that plane takes off to break up the circus performances. I'm sure they'll do a good job at gathering information. I think the Horribles would do a good job too, since most of them have done detective work."

"Then why didn't you ask us, instead of Sniffy, who has never done any such work before?" 18 asked.

"That's a fair question," Freddy said. "I guess the only answer is, you didn't happen to be around." He thought for a minute. "However," he said, "if we had twice as many spies at the field, we'd get twice as much information, and if you rabbits want to go, I'll drop you off at the same time. Wait, wait!" he said, as the Horribles began whacking one another on the back and shouting "Hurray!" "There are two conditions: one, that you forget this quarrel— and that goes for you Wilsons, too. You can work as separate outfits, but there's to be no rivalry, and you must share all the information you get. Agreed?"

They agreed readily enough, and Sniffy went up and clasped paws with the Head Horrible, and the others shook paws all around. Then Freddy told them the other condition. It was that the Horribles supply their own parachutes.

This wasn't so easy, but Freddy was sure that since it was something that was going to help Mr. Boomschmidt, Uncle Ben would be willing to drive around the neighborhood and collect old umbrellas. And if he couldn't find enough, Mrs. Bean would run up a few chutes on her sewing machine.

So then the outlaws and the Horribles formed up in two lines, facing each other, and Sniffy and No. 18 stepped out in front and put their paws on each other's shoulders and kissed each other on both cheeks, like French generals, and then both sides joined in a cheer, and turned Right face! and marched off in different directions.

*So then the Outlaws and the Horribles formed
two lines and kissed each other.*

When Freddy came down to the barnyard next morning, Mr. Bean was harnessing Hank up to the buggy, to drive in to Centerboro. Freddy hesitated a minute. He knew that although Mr. Bean was very proud of his talking animals he really didn't like to hear them talk. He was the same way about the telephone. It embarrassed him somehow to hear a voice coming out of the wall, and it made him nervous to know that he was expected to give some kind of an answer. And so when his phone rang he always pretended not to hear it. In the same way, it was easier to pretend that an animal had not spoken, than to admit that a horse or a pig had opened its mouth and given out perfectly good English words.

But Mr. Bean had got so he didn't object so much to hearing Freddy speak as he did when wild animals, like squirrels and woodchucks, who had picked up the habit from farm animals, said things in his hearing. So Freddy said: "Want me to take you in the plane?"

Mr. Bean looked at him a minute, then he jerked his head towards the corner of the barn, and when Freddy had followed him around out of sight of Hank, he put his hand on the pig's shoulder and bent down. "Like to," he whispered. "But can't. Hurt Hank's feelings."

Hank was the one who always took Mr. Bean in to Centerboro. He might feel bad if Mr. Bean went with Freddy in his new plane. "That's right," Freddy said. "But how about a ride before you go into town. Only half an hour or so."

"Good!" said Mr. Bean, and when he'd told Hank to wait for him at the front gate, they went out and got in the plane. Then Mr. Wogus swung the propeller for them and they were off.

Freddy went up first to five thousand feet and swung in a circle so that Mr. Bean could get a good general view of his part of the state. Then he came down and flew low over the farm and the Big Woods, the Macy and Witherspoon farms, and Centerboro. At first Freddy had heard, above the noise of the engine, a queer wailing sound. It worried him. He looked at his instruments, and then he looked up and down the sideways, but everything seemed in order. And then he turned and looked back at his passenger. Mr. Bean's mouth was wide open and his Adam's apple was sliding up and down, and

Freddy realized that something unheard of was happening. Mr. Bean was singing.

Mr. Bean was pretty conservative. That is, he didn't like what he called new-fangled things— automobiles and telephones and radios and such. In Centerboro, when he walked past Beller & Rohr's, he turned his head away so that he wouldn't see the television set in the window. But somehow he had seemed to feel that an airplane was all right. And now Freddy was delighted to see that he was really enjoying the ride. The next time Freddy turned around he winked at him and went right on singing.

When they came down Mrs. Bean was waiting at the edge of the pasture. "Land sakes, Mr. B.," she said, "you scared the wits out of me. Tearing around the sky, at your age!"

"Now, now, Mrs. B.," he said, "take it easy. With the best pilot in the state, I'm safe in that plane as I'd be in church. Safer, maybe. Might fall off to sleep in church and bump my nose on a pew back."

"That's no way to talk," she said severely. "I suppose you'll tell me next you enjoyed it."

"So I did," he replied. "Saw Macy, putting a

new roof on his barn. Witherspoon's awful late with his work, as usual. Mrs. W., she's trying to clean up her garden, pullin' and cat-haulin' at it with a busted rake. Couple of Schermerhorn's cows got over the wall into our daisy lot, and both Witherspoon's and Schermerhorn's fences could do with a little work."

Mrs. Bean sniffed. "Trust you to see nothing from the sky that you don't see every day on the ground. Send you around the world and all you'd have to tell would be how some Fiji Islander couldn't plough a straight furrow."

"Oh, I dunno," said Mr. Bean. "There was the lake all blue and sparklin' like millions of sapphires, and beyond it the woods like a soft green velvet carpet, and down on this side of it the little fields all different colors and cut up every which way, and the roads sneaking through and past them and sliding between the hills and through the villages with their little doll house. Eleven steeples I counted."

"Like me to take you up, Mrs. Bean?" Freddy asked.

"No, sir!" she said. "You'll never get me into one of those contraptions." But Freddy saw how her black eyes were snapping with excitement, and he wasn't surprised when she said: "Besides I just put a cake in the oven."

"Guess you could trust me to take it out, Mrs. B.," Mr. Bean said.

She looked at him a minute. "Guess I'll have to," she said. "If I'm not back by ten-fifteen, take it out. How do you get into this thing, Freddy?"

So they helped her into her seat and saw that her safety belt was fastened. Then Freddy got in. Mr. Bean called, "Switch off?" and when Freddy called back, "Switch off!" he went up to the propeller, and swung it a few times, then called "Contact!" "Contact!" Freddy shouted, and Mr. Bean swung again and the engine started with a roar.

They had circled twice at different altitudes when Mrs. Bean tapped Freddy on the shoulder. Freddy said into his microphone: "Everything all right?" but then he turned and saw that she didn't have her head phones on. He pointed to them, but she shook her head. Evidently she didn't want to put them on. She raised one hand and slid it around, imitating a plane doing stunts. "For goodness' sake!"

Freddy thought, and he imitated her movement, looking at her inquiringly. She nodded vigorously.

So after seeing that Mrs. Bean's safety belt was securely fastened, Freddy went up to four thousand and did a wing over. He looked around; she smiled at him and made the motion of clapping her hands. "Golly, she likes it," he thought. So then he went on and did loops and rolls and Immelmanns—all the stunts that he was sure he could do skilfully, and every time he turned to see how Mrs. Bean was taking it, she was laughing happily.

At last they came down, and Mr. Bean ran out to meet them. "Freddy," he said, "what in tarnation do you mean by taking Mrs. Bean up there and bouncing her all over the sky! You remember, I gave you this plane and I can take it back again."

"Oh, now, calm yourself, Mr. B.," Mrs. Bean said. "Freddy was just doing what I told him to."

"Well, you hadn't ought to have told him. My heart was in my mouth the whole endurin' time."

"You won't have any of that cake in your

mouth, if you don't take it out of the oven,"
Mrs. Bean said. "So you put your heart back in
your chest and go in and—no, I can smell it;
it's too late. You've let it burn. If you'd done as
I told you to—"

Mr. Bean started to say something, and then
he stopped and just shook his head. He knew it
was no use arguing with Mrs. Bean, particularly
as she had Freddy to back her up. And he hadn't
really been scared on her account anyway. He
just thought that it didn't do any harm to let
her think that he had worried about her. And
maybe he was a little put out that Freddy hadn't
done any stunts when he had gone up with him.
Mrs. Bean had got ahead of him again. She usually did. He smiled to himself as she hurried
back to the house to take the burnt cake out of
the oven.

CHAPTER

11

That night Freddy dropped twenty-four spies on the secret airfield—nine skunks and fifteen rabbits. It was not an easy operation. Of course they didn't weigh much, and so could be dropped from as low as a hundred feet. But to get the umbrellas up and manage to have them jump so that they would clear the tail of the plane was a slow job, and he had to make three runs across the field before they were all out.

He knew that whoever was with the plane would certainly come out to see what was going on, and would notice the umbrellas floating down; so he waited until one in the morning before starting. As it happened, someone did come running out of the house, which stood a hundred yards back of the barn, and turned a spotlight on and swept it across the sky. But by that time all the spies were down, and as there were trees between him and the field, he couldn't have seen the rabbits and skunks putting down their umbrellas and running for cover even if he'd turned the light that way.

"I'll give you two days," Freddy had told them. "Then I'll either come, or send somebody, to get your report. Keep watch for me by the big elm at the northeast corner of the field."

Mr. Condiment did not return to Centerboro, but his lawyer, Mr. Newsome did. He took a room at the hotel and went out to see Mr. Boomschmidt and Mademoiselle Rose.

"My client, Mr. Watson P. Condiment," he

said, "wishes me to tell you that he is not, and never has been, engaged to this Miss Del Pardo. He does not know, and has never before in his life even seen Miss Del Pardo."

"Gracious me," said Mr. Boomschmidt, "that is very strange, 'since he has written a whole series of comic books about her."

"My client did not write the books," said Mr. Newsome. "A Mr. Gizling wrote them."

"Funny name, Gizling," Mr. Boomschmidt said. "But so's Boomschmidt, for that matter. Newsome, now—that's a nice name. Too bad it's so like Nuisance, though. Must make you very sad when you think of it."

"My client," said Mr. Newsome, "feels that he has been very patient with Mademoiselle Rose and with you. But he has reached the end of his patience. He wishes me to warn you that if within three days Mademoiselle Rose does not agree to marry him, he intends to take much more drastic measures."

"Drastic, drastic?" said Mr. Boomschmidt thoughtfully. "I'm afraid I don't know what kind of a measure that is. You see, I just learned in school the ordinary measures, like four cups one pint, two pints one gallon, and so on."

"That's wrong," said Mr. Newsome irritably. "It's two cups one pint, two pints one quart."

"Really?" said Mr. Boomschmidt doubtfully. "Are you sure? We'd better ask Leo. Leo!" he called, and when the lion came over to where they were standing, he said: "Look, Leo, how many quarts to a pint, do you remember?"

"It's not quarts to a pint!" Mr. Newsome snapped. "It's two pints to a quart."

"Don't ask me, chief," Leo said. "I've got no head for figures."

"Well, I have," Mr. Boomschmidt said. "I've a very good head for 'em. It's just that I can't always remember 'em. They're *in* my head, you understand, but I can't always get 'em out. Like—"

"Look, Mr. Boomschmidt," Mr. Newsome interrupted. "Mr. Condiment wants—"

"Like twelve inches one yard," Mr. Boomschmidt went right on; "three yards one foot—"

"It is twelve inches one *foot!*" Mr. Newsome fairly shouted. It evidently irritated him so much to hear Mr. Boomschmidt get everything wrong that until he had set him right he couldn't go on with what he wanted to say. "And it's three feet one yard."

"No!" said Mr. Boomschmidt wonderingly. "Are you sure? Dear me, I've got all those things down in a little book somewhere. Not that I doubt you, Mr. Newsome. But take miles now, —there are quite a lot of inches in them, and goodness knows how many feet. And then I'd like to look up that drastic measurement, too. I tell you what—you stay to supper, and—"

Nobody could talk to Mr. Boomschmidt and keep his temper if Mr. Boomschmidt wanted him to lose it. Mr. Newsome lost his completely at this point. He turned very red and jumped up and down with anger. "If you'll just *let* me I wish to *tell* you what Mr. Condiment *said*," he yelled.

"Oh, does Mr. Condiment know about miles and inches?" Mr. Boomschmidt asked mildly. "Well, that's very kind of him to help us out, but as I told you, I have it all down in a little book, and—"

"A-a-a-ach!" said Mr. Newsome disgustedly, and he turned around and started for the gate. Mr. Boomschmidt winked and nodded at Leo, and the lion walked slowly after him. Mr. Newsome looked over his shoulder and walked a little faster, and Leo walked a little faster too.

Then Mr. Newsome started to run. Leo broke into a canter. The gate was closed, and by the time Mr. Newsome reached it he was running much too fast to be able to stop and open it. Leo didn't think he could jump it, either, for it was five feet high. "Guess I'd better help him," he thought, and when Mr. Newsome was a few yards from the gate the lion opened his jaws and let out a full-throated roar. Mr. Newsome sailed into the air and cleared the gate by a good foot.

"That was fun, chief," Leo said. "But it didn't get us anywhere."

"It got Brother Newsome somewhere," said his employer. "And he's still going. I figure about fifteen feet to the yard, the speed he's making."

"I heard him tell about those drastic measures," said Leo. "I wish you'd let him tell what they are."

"He wouldn't tell us," Mr. Boomschmidt said. "Condiment's up to something all right, but he won't want us to be ready for whatever it is. I think we'll have Hannibal and the other elephants go on all night guard duty. He's pretty likely to hire some thugs to cut the tent ropes or something like that."

Mr. Newsome sailed into the air.

"I don't think Freddy has accomplished much," said the lion.

"Oh, now, I wouldn't say that, Leo. He's found where that plane is kept. As soon as those spies of his report, we can probably complain to the state police and have the pilot arrested. With luck we might get enough on Condiment to put him in jail. But at any rate Freddy has scared Condiment away from Centerboro."

"I'd like to know what Condiment thinks about that leopard business. He can't really believe that Lorna the Leopard Woman walked right out of his story."

"He probably thinks that there really is a leopard woman, and that that writer, Gizling, wrote the stories about her," Mr. Boomschmidt said. "Freddy's idea isn't bad, you know. He's trying to scare Condiment into marrying Lorna, just as Condiment is trying to scare Rose into marrying him. I mean, the one that loses out will be the one that gets the scaredest. Oh dear, it's not the unmanageable animals that give us trouble, it's the unmanageable people."

"You can say 'unmanageable' all right now, chief," Leo remarked.

Mr. Boomschmidt winked at him. "Just be-

between you and me, Leo, when I want to I can
even say 'Theophilus Thistle, the thistle sifter,'
and all the rest of it."

Now that the mysterious plane had been lo-
cated, it was no longer necessary to have performances, and the circus animals had another
vacation. Freddy stayed at home and spent most
of his time working with the Benjamin Bean
Self-filling Piggy Bank. It was really too clumsy
a contraption for one animal to lug around,
since he would have had to walk along, holding
it up and looking in the eyepiece at the same
time. The way they worked it, two animals carried it, and they hired one of the mice to sit on
top and look in the eyepiece.

They found several dollars' worth of coins
and a great collection of odds and ends of metal
of all kinds. They found an old sword with the
blade nearly rusted away, and a queer gold ring,
which Georgie insisted was a magic ring. He
spent hours rubbing it, but no genie ever appeared. Finally he gave it to Mrs. Bean. She
wore it for quite a long time.

Freddy wanted to work some of the other
farm gardens, and even those in Centerboro.
He said they could make a deal with the owners

—give them half of what they found. But Uncle Ben said better wait, he didn't want people to know about it yet. "Mobs," he said. "Worse than World Series."

"I suppose you're right," said Freddy. "Everybody in the country would be crowded into the front yard, trying to buy one." So he warned all the animals not to talk about it.

But word about it got out anyway. One day Lyman, the muskrat, dropped in. He had as usual half a dozen damp comics under his arm. "Where's Sniffy?" he asked.

Mrs. Wiggins said he was away on a visit.

Lyman looked around curiously. "What's this thing for finding hidden treasure I hear so much talk about?" he asked.

"What sort of nonsense have you been listening to?" said Mrs. Wiggins.

But Lyman just grinned at her. "I thought I'd like to borrow it for a while," he said. "I know where there's a lot of gold coins buried."

"You'd better go dig 'em up then," the cow said.

"I can't dig up a whole—" Lyman stopped short. "I don't know exactly where they are," he said.

"Well, even if we had such a machine," the cow began—

"Every animal within twenty miles knows you've got it," Lyman said. "They know Uncle Ben invented it, and they know you've been using it in the garden. I'll give you half of what I find."

Mrs. Wiggins shook her head. "You'd better go see Uncle Ben."

So Lyman went up into the loft where Uncle Ben was working. Pretty soon he came out again, and he was mad. "All right!" he said angrily as he came down the stairs. "All right! You keep your old piggy bank. You won't keep it long, I can tell you!"

"Now, now," said Mrs. Wiggins. "What did he say, Lyman?"

"Said he wasn't manufacturing them yet. Said when he was, I would be free to buy one just like everybody else. Said until then, they weren't on the market."

"Well, you can't very well buy 'em until they're made," said the cow.

"He's got one. And all I wanted to do was to borrow it for a day," said Lyman. "But O K, if he wants to be mean, I can be mean too." He grinned at Mrs. Wiggins. "Just let him wait and see!"

Mrs. Wiggins laughed her comfortable laugh. "Why Lyman, you look quite villainous! I bet you're thinking up something pretty awful to do! Maybe put a thumb tack in Uncle Ben's chair."

Lyman didn't answer. He hurried off. He was in such a rush that he forgot his comics, which Mrs. Wiggins picked up and carried into the cow barn with her.

Later in the day there were such shouts of laughter coming out of the cow barn that Freddy went in to investigate. When Mrs. Wiggins laughed, you could hear her for a couple of miles on a clear day. But when she and her two sisters got to laughing, shingles began to fly off the barn roof. It was some time before they could stop enough to tell Freddy what it was all about, and they wouldn't have stopped even then if Mr. Bean hadn't become alarmed for the roof. He came hurrying in. "Consarn it!" he shouted. "You tryin' to wreck my farm? I like a good joke as well as the next one but I don't laugh so hard over 'em I destroy property."

After they'd quieted down and Mr. Bean had gone, they told Freddy they were laughing at Lyman's comics.

Freddy said: "Why, I've seen some that were sort of funny, but not as funny as that."

"Oh, it isn't the funny ones we're laughing at," Mrs. Wurzburger said. "The funny ones make us cry. It's the awful ones that are really funny—the ones that are supposed to scare you. This about The Demon Woman of Grisly Gulch. She's got horns and a tail. My gracious, Sister Wogus, maybe you're The Demon Woman!" And she began to laugh and put a hoof over her mouth.

"You'd better take that stuff up into the woods," Freddy said. "Mr. Bean will be mad if you get to laughing again."

So the three cows took the comics up into the woods. They were hollering and laughing over them up there all the rest of the day. Three squirrels were injured by being shaken out of trees when the cows found a specially horrid comic.

CHAPTER
12

It was next morning that General Grimm and his staff came back. Freddy saw the big plane circling down towards the pasture when he came out after breakfast. He ran down to the workshop to warn Uncle Ben.

Uncle Ben grinned. He pulled a handful of

quarters out of his pocket. "Get up there and scatter these over the ground around your plane. Hurry up before they land. I'll bring the bombsight."

When the officers climbed out of their plane and walked over to where Freddy was taking the canvas cover off his engine, Uncle Ben was walking slowly up and down beside him, squinting in the eyepiece of the Self-filling Piggy Bank and stooping every now and then to pick something off the ground.

"Mr. Bean!" General Grimm snapped.

Uncle Ben looked up and smiled. "Morning, General." Then he went back to the Piggy Bank.

General Grimm pointed to Freddy's plane. "No preparation!" he shouted. "Army's time wasted! Outrageous!"

Colonel Tablet said: "The General feels that since you were notified that we wished another test of the bombsight, you should be ready for us. I see neither bombs nor bombsight."

Uncle Ben stopped an picked up a quarter which he held out to the Colonel. But General Grimm seized his arm. "What's this?" he demanded. "Bribing my officers?"

"Found it," said Uncle Ben. "With bomb-sight. Walk along, look in eyepiece, flicker-flicker, money on ground." He illustrated, picked up another quarter then held out the bombsight to the General. "Try it."

The General crooked a finger. "Tablet!" he said, and Col. Tablet took the Piggy Bank and began walking along, peering in the eyepiece. He stopped, leaned down, and picked up a coin. The other officers followed along, watching closely. When he picked up the second quarter, General Grimm held out his hand. "I'll take those," he said.

"Sorry, sir," said the Colonel, and slid the coins in his pocket.

"Tablet!" roared the General, but Col. Drosky said: "Let me try it, sir. I'll split with you, fifty-fifty."

"Split, nothing!" said General Grimm. "Work it myself." And he tried to take the Piggy Bank from the Colonel.

They were both trying to pull it away from each other when General Grumby laid a hand on General Grimm's shoulder. "Better let me try it, Grimm," he said. "Machine looks danger-ous to me—may be a bomb. We can't risk our most capable general's life for twenty-five cents."

"Well," said General Grimm doubtfully, but he gave up. General Grumby started off with the Piggy Bank.

"Excuse me, sir," said Col. Queeck, who had been exchanging a few whispered words with one of the other officers. "I don't think any general should risk his life in such a dangerous test. Even colonels, if I may say so, sir, are too valuable. But Major Jampers here has offered to try out this machine. Would you let him have it, sir?"

"If you please, sir," said the Major, stepping forward, "I'm really very happy to take the risk for you. And you know, sir, I'm really not a very good major; no loss at all to the army if I get blown up."

"With all respect, sir," said Colonel Drosky, stepping up and saluting General Grimm, "I believe I would be even less loss than Jampers. You told me two days ago that I was a disgrace to the service—remember?" He made a grab at the Piggy Bank.

Four of them now had their hands on the Piggy Bank and were pulling at it. Colonel

Drosky jabbed Major Jampers in the ribs with his elbow, and Colonel Queeck and Colonel Drosky started trying to shove each other away, and General Grumby tried to kick Colonel Tablet, and then General Grimm, who had been standing back, took a short run into the middle of the struggling group. And the Benjamin Bean Self-filling Piggy Bank fell to the ground with a smash.

The scuffle stopped, and the officers fell back and watched Uncle Ben as he picked up the Piggy Bank and examined it.

"Busted," he said after a minute, and started back towards the barnyard.

But they ran after him and surrounded him. "Want to order one," said General Grimm.

"Me too." "And me." "I'll take two." They all talked at once. "How soon can we get them? How much will they be?"

"Six weeks," said Uncle Ben. "Thousand dollars."

They all stopped talking. There was silence for a minute, then Colonel Tablet said: "There are eight of us here, counting Captain Gilpin and Lieutenant Flapp over there in the plane. If we all chip in and buy one—form a club—"

"I think generals ought to chip in more than the lower ranks," said Major Jampers.

"Right!" said Colonel Queeck. "Generals, three hundred. Other ranks, h'm—six goes into four hundred—"

"But majors—" Jampers began.

Freddy had been so interested that he hadn't noticed a large figure which was toiling up the slope from the barnyard. But as the man climbed clumsily over the lower wall, Freddy saw him and ran to meet him. Only something very important would make Mr. Ollie Groper take so much exercise.

Groper leaned panting against the wall and mopped his face. "Hope this here peregrination . . . have no deleterious effect . . . my accustomed salubrity," he gasped. "Shall endeavor . . . achieve brevity." He paused, then said hastily, and in a different tone: "You know a muskrat named Lyman?" Having said which he looked embarrassed, no doubt at having used so many ordinary words.

"Sure," said Freddy. "Friend of Sniffy Wilson's. Lives down on the flats."

Mr. Groper was getting his breath back. "Would it astonish and perplex you to learn that this Lyman and that there eminent jurist, Mr. Montague Newsome, are involved in some nefarious intrigue?"

"Lyman?" said Freddy. "Oh, I can't believe—"

"Allow me to conclude my narration," said Mr. Groper. It took some time, but at the end of it Freddy was in possession of some curious facts. Lyman had come into the hotel and asked for Mr. Newsome. Mr. Groper had naturally been somewhat surprised to have a muskrat come up to the desk and ask for a guest, but he had given Lyman Mr. Newsome's room number. Lyman had gone up in the elevator, and after about an hour he and the lawyer had come down. Mr. Newsome had made two long distance telephone calls, and then he and Lyman had got in his car and driven off.

But the important thing was what Mr. Groper had overheard. It had been hot in the telephone booth in the lobby, and by the end of his second call Mr. Newsome was perspiring heavily and hardly able to breathe. So he had opened the door, and Mr. Groper had heard him say: "No, don't fly to the field. It's only four miles to West Nineveh, and there's a field there.

Mr. Groper had naturally been somewhat surprised.

I'll meet you there with the car. That way you won't attract too much attention." There was silence for a minute or so, and then he said: "According to the information I have, it does work on silver, gold and copper. And it will be easy to get." Then he hung up. "You think it was Condiment he was talking to?" Freddy asked.

"Consideration of all the circumstances confirms that conclusion," Mr. Groper agreed.

"I think so too," said the pig. "And they're after the Piggy Bank, as well as Mademoiselle Rose. But I don't see . . . ." He thought a minute. "Condiment is going to fly from Philadelphia up to West Ninevah, and Newsome will pick him up there and drive to their secret airfield. They'll come down here and try to steal the Piggy Bank. But if I know Condiment, he'll send someone else to do that job—he won't come himself. That means that when whoever he sends starts for the farm, Condiment will probably be alone at the airfield. I guess that's my chance." He glanced around at the army officers who were still pressing in a tight group around Uncle Ben, shouting and waving their arms as they wrangled about how much each should pay towards the Piggy Bank. "Guess I'll have to fly to Centerboro first. I'd take you, only I expect you've got your car."

"Aerial locomotion," said Mr. Groper, "ain't among my desiderata. I got a predilection for terrene ambulation. So while in the vicinity, guess I'll indulge in a colloquy with the estimable Beans."

Freddy thanked him as they walked down towards the house. At the back porch they parted, and Freddy went in to see Mrs. Wiggins. First he drew her a map of the secret airfield. It looked like this:

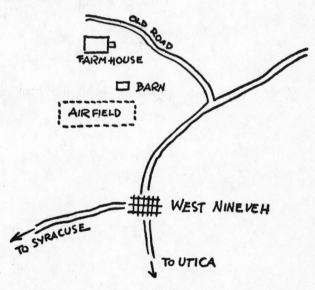

"I'm leaving you this just in case," he said. "I can't tell you my plans, because I haven't really got any yet. I'm just going scouting. But if you don't hear from me in three or four days, maybe you'd better send—let me see, J. J. Pomeroy's a pretty slow flyer, even for a robin, but he's dependable. Yes, send him up to look around."

CHAPTER
13

When Sniffy and his merry men, and the Horrible Ten—who were really the Horrible Fifteen—floated down on to the secret air strip, they hurriedly folded up their umbrellas and made for the woods on the south side of the field, for the searchlight at the farmhouse was poking sharp fingers through the foliage, feeling for intruders. Once under cover they held a whispered council of war, and then, having hidden the umbrellas in a hollow tree, lay down and went to sleep.

In the morning Sniffy and No. 18 posted their men around the barn and the farmhouse, and along the old road. Every two hours they made the rounds. Aroma and Sniffy, Jr., dug a hole under the foundation on the west side of the house behind some bushes. They found that there was no cellar, and they managed to get in under the floor of the room which the occupants used as a living room.

There were two men in the house: the plane's pilot, Jackson, and a mechanic named Felix. Much of their talk was technical stuff about the plane, and the skunks didn't understand it. They quarreled a good deal. Felix did the cooking, and Jackson didn't think much of it. They quarreled much more bitterly over the games of slap jack that they spent most of their time playing. Jackson had a terrible temper, and slap jack isn't a game for people who can't control themselves. When a jack was played, and they both tried to slap it at once, they would of course slap each other. Some of the games just ended up in seeing who could slap the hardest.

Rabbit No. 23, who was an ex-Head Horrible, managed to hop up on the windowsill one evening. He reported that the room was comfortably furnished, although not as elegantly as Mrs. Bean's parlor, since there was no photograph album on the center table and no picture of Washington Crossing the Delaware on the wall. But there was a rack containing several guns beside the door. No. 23 felt that they should get into the house somehow and either steal the guns or do something to render them useless. But before their plans were made, Jackson came back from West Nineveh, where he went twice a week to telephone, with word that "the boss" was coming next day. The boss, the animals were sure, could be no one but Mr. Condiment.

Nothing had been heard from Freddy, and they had no way of getting word to him. They kept watch by the big elm, but Mr. Pomeroy didn't appear. What had happened, they learned later, was that J. J. had set out from the farm the day after Freddy dropped them over the field. But in a thunderstorm his spectacles, which he now had to wear all the time, blew off. He flew on, since any attempt to find them would be useless, but as the weather did not clear he couldn't see his landmarks, and he flew west instead of north. He got nearly to Buffalo before he found out where he was.

"We've got to do *something*," Sniffy said. "You don't think Robin Hood would have just sat around like this, do you?"

"My Horribles are restless too," said 18. "But we can't attack. I tell you what. There's a loose board in the kitchen floor." And he outlined a plan.

That evening Felix and Jackson sat down to their nightly game of slap jack. Halfway through dealing the cards Jackson stopped and raised his head. "What's that?" They pushed back their chairs and went to the door.

A rabbit can give a shrill high-pitched scream that sounds pretty scary at night. When six rabbits all start screaming together, the effect is just plain terrifying. And six of the Horribles were down by the barn, screaming their heads off. The men ran back and pulled guns out of the rack, and sneaked cautiously down towards the terrible sounds.

Sniffy and Aroma and Sniffy, Jr., and the other nine rabbits were under the kitchen floor. The rest of the Wilsons were posted in the bushes near the house door with bows strung and arrows nocked to the strings, ready to create a diversion if the men came back too soon.

But the six Horribles moved slowly off down the old road, screaming at intervals, and drawing the men after them; so that the raiders were able to accomplish what they had set out to do. They lifted the loose board and scrambled up into the house. Ten minutes later when word that the men were returning was relayed to them from outside, they had succeeded in getting two shotguns down from the rack, and in dragging them out through the hole under the floor. Sniffy had also brought out three boxes of shotgun shells. And the men were so interested in wondering what the screaming could have been that they never noticed that the guns were gone.

A shotgun isn't much use to a rabbit or a skunk. "Even if we could get the muzzle up to aim," No. 4 said, "the thing would kick us right into the middle of next Sunday at supper time. I vote we bury 'em."

"We'll put 'em in the tree with the umbrellas," said No. 18. "They may come in handy. Bring those cartridges along. We've got work to do at the barn."

There were plenty of holes in the barn; they had gone in it the first day and inspected the plane, and tried vainly to figure out some way of putting it out of commission. Now they went in, and when they had gnawed off the ends of the cartridges and got the powder out, Sniffy laid a train of it from under the plane out through a hole and along the ground for five or six yards. Then he went in and turned the spigot on a big iron barrel of gasoline. He watched until the gasoline had formed a pool under the plane and had touched the powder train, then he went out, leaving the spigot open.

And found that nobody had a match.

"You know that Mr. Bean won't allow us to have matches," No. 7 said. "He's afraid we'll burn the barn down."

"Well, here's one barn he'll be glad to have

us burn," said Sniffy. "Oh, darn it, how can we get a match?"

"I saw some in the kitchen," said Sniffy, Jr.

His father looked at him for a minute. Then he said: "Wait right here." He ran back to the house. He crawled under the kitchen, lifted the board, and crept cautiously over to the stove. The matches were in a holder hung on a nail a good foot out of Sniffy's reach. He saw a yard stick in a corner of the room, so he got it and, holding it between his paws, pushed one end up under the match holder and jiggled it. Nothing happened. He jiggled it harder, and the matches jumped around, but none came out. He jiggled it harder, and the whole holder came off the nail and dropped.

It rattled on the floor, but luckily for Sniffy, at that moment in the next room Felix dealt a jack, and the bang as both men slapped at it covered the sound. Sniffy grabbed half a dozen matches in his mouth and ducked down under the floor.

"Everybody here?" he said, when he had rejoined the others.

"All present and accounted for," said 18.

"Then scatter," he said. "You know what to do. Get as far away as possible." And when they had gone he touched a match to the powder train and ran.

He stopped on the far side of the clearing and watched. A bright light and a plume of white smoke traveled along the powder train. It looked like a little steam engine as it went up to the barn, through the hole, and then . . . whoosh!—there was a gush of flame, and boom! —the sides of the barn blew apart and the roof opened up like a book. In two minutes the barn wasn't a barn any longer, and the plane itself was burning fiercely.

Mr. Condiment had chosen the site of his secret airfield well. Lying in a fold of the hills, it was so well hidden from observation that nobody saw the flames. Nobody notified the West Nineveh fire department—who in any case couldn't have done anything. And Felix and Jackson could only stand and watch until the barn had burned to the ground and the plane was a scorched skeleton.

The Horribles and the Wilsons watched from the other side of the field. They laughed and danced and whacked one another on the back as

He touched a match to the powder train.

the flames roared up, and when at last they died
down, 18 said: "Well, Brother Horribles,
there's a good night's work done. And all thanks
to Sniffy. Let's give him the Horrible salute."

So the rabbits began circling around Sniffy
in a war dance, and sang:

O Sniffy, we salute you,
And hereby constitute you
A Horrible (first class) and we
Do therefore solemnly agree
To back you up in any fight.
Provided you're not in the right.
But in the wrong, we'll stand by you.
(Good deeds of course, we never do.)
If you have enemies, we'll help
To make them holler, squirm and yelp;
We'll pinch them black, we'll punch them blue!
Oh, we'll do anything for you!"

Sniffy was pleased, and he thanked them; but
later he said to Aroma: "Robin Hood was a
fighter; he didn't go in for sabotage. Oh, sure;
we had to do it for Mr. Boom. But I didn't like
doing it much."

"Oh, Sniff, don't be silly," said his wife.

"Robin Hood didn't have gunpowder; if he had, he'd have blown that Sheriff of Nottingham right through the roof of his old castle."

Sniffy dreamt of noble deeds and rescues all night, and when he woke in the morning the contrast between the heroic exploits he had dreamed of and just setting fire to an old barn made him feel unhappy. But he cheered up when he saw the new respect with which the Horribles greeted him. Even his own children were respectful. This is very unusual among young skunks.

Late in the morning a car came bumping up the old road. It stopped by the barn and the animals, watching from their posts, saw Mr. Condiment and Mr. Newsome get out. The men just stared silently at the ruins of the barn. After a minute Felix and Jackson came out from the house, and then Mr. Condiment let loose. He yelled and roared and stamped his feet; he called them every name he could think of, and accused and threatened until his voice gave out, and then he kept right on in a whisper. He didn't give them a chance to explain, which was just as well for them, since they didn't have any explanation. And finally even the whisper gave out, and Mr. Newsome said: "Let's go back to the car and talk it over."

The animals couldn't get near enough to hear anything, but the argument seemed less angry now that Mr. Condiment was silent. The others talked, and he chewed throat lozenges and wrote notes in a little book which he then passed around. Finally they all got out and went over to the house to have some lunch. And it was while they were there that Freddy came sliding down from the sky in his plane and made an elegant three-point landing on the field.

CHAPTER

14

In landing on the secret field, Freddy had expected to be received with suspicion, perhaps to be warned off with threats, and he had a story ready. He was amazed to have Mr. Condiment rush up to him as he climbed out and practically throw his arms around him. "My dear sir! This is delightful, charming—I mean to say, very pleasing. You are more than welcome, sir. Perhaps you can help us out of a dilemma."

"I must apologize," Freddy said. "The oil pressure dropped suddenly and I saw this field and decided I'd better set her down and see what is wrong. Was on my way to pick up a passenger in Oswego and fly him to Washington."

"You're in luck," said Mr. Condiment. "Felix here is an excellent mechanic. He can find the trouble. While he's looking it over, come down to the house. I have a proposition for you.—Good heavens, what's that—a cat?" For Jinx was sitting in the passenger's seat of the plane.

"My mascot," said Freddy. "Devoted to me—always goes along. Very affectionate little fellow —aren't you, kitty-witty?" he said in a sugary voice.

Jinx gave him a dirty look and turned his back and began to wash his face.

On the way to the house Freddy glanced at the ruins of the barn. "That must have been a bad fire," he said. "Was it recent?"

"Yes. That's what I want to talk to you about. You see, it is important, vital—that is, necessary, that I fly to a certain place tonight. Well, I have

my pilot, but no plane. It burned last night. —
Yes?" he said to Felix, who had come running
after them. "What is it?"

"That cat," Felix said. "He won't let me
touch your plane, mister."

So Freddy went back. Jackson was saying:
"Come, kitty, nice kitty!" and trying to coax
Jinx out. Jinx just arched his back and spit.

"Here, here," said Freddy. "Get out. This
man is going to look at my oil line." He saw that
for some reason Jinx didn't want to get out, but
neither of them could say anything in front of
the men. And as Freddy persisted, Jinx finally
jumped out and sat down under the wing and
went on washing his face.

Freddy went back to the house. "Come in-
side," said Mr. Condiment. "And do take off
that helmet and those goggles."

But Freddy said no, he was so accustomed to
wearing them that he didn't feel properly
dressed without them on. So then Mr. Condiment made his proposition. He would pay two
hundred dollars for the use of Freddy's plane
that night.

Freddy said, "I agree. Only I must fly the
plane myself."

This of course didn't suit Mr. Condiment at all, and they were arguing about it when Jackson came into the room. He tossed what looked like a bundle of clothes on the table. "Take a look at that," he said. And Freddy jumped up. For the bundle was wrapped in a black skirt, and it unrolled as it struck the table, and out fell a shawl, a flat black hat, high-heeled shoes, some castanets, and an artificial rose.

Mr. Condiment jumped up too. "Where did you find that?" he demanded.

"In this guy's plane."

Freddy was horrified. So that was why Jinx hadn't wanted to get out! He had remembered the costume was there and was afraid Felix would find it. "And I forgot it!" Freddy thought. "Oh, gosh, I'd better get out of here!" But he was too late. They grabbed him as he edged around the table. In the scuffle the helmet and goggles came off.

"Hey, it's a pig!" shouted Felix.

"What?" Mr. Condiment exclaimed. "Newsome! Where's Newsome? He told me about this creature, this animal—I mean, this pig. Yes, yes; he's a friend of old Boomschmidt's. He's smart, he's got brains—that is, he's dangerous.

"Hey—it's a pig!"

And that costume—ha, I see now! Lorna, eh?"
He pushed his face close to Freddy's and did
something that Freddy had read about in books
but had never seen done—he gnashed his teeth.
"So *you* were Lorna!" he snarled. "Well, Lorna,
take that!" And he slapped Freddy's face hard
twice.

Pigs don't have as sensitive skins as people do,
but their feelings are just as easily hurt. "He
slapped me because I am a pig," he thought. "If
I were a boy or a man he wouldn't have done it."
It made Freddy feel bad, but he was mad too.
He was mad at himself for his carelessness. But
he told himself that he wasn't mad at Mr. Condiment. He would defeat Mr. Condiment; he
would return those slaps, and add a couple of
kicks for good measure, when he got the chance,
but he thought, "I am *not* going to lose my temper! Mr. Bean had told him once, "If you lose
your temper in a fight you're licked before you
start." And Freddy believed that it was true.

They tied him up and gagged him and shoved
him into a dark closet off the kitchen and locked
the door. He wasn't really very uncomfortable.
If he had been a thin pig the cords and the hard
boards and the gag would have hurt more; but

as he said later, he always carried his own cush-
ions around with him. Of course his thoughts
weren't very pleasant. And after a long time he
began to get pretty stiff and to ache a lot.

Hours later he heard the engine of his plane.
It started with a roar, then sank to a hum as
someone ran it to warm it up, then roared again
and gradually died away. Then for a long time
nothing happened. Freddy couldn't do anything but worry. So he worried.

But quite a lot was happening outside. As
soon as Freddy's plane, with Jackson at the controls and Felix in the seat behind, had dwindled
and disappeared in the darkening southern
sky, the Wilsons and the Horribles closed in on
the house. Mr. Condiment and Mr. Newsome,
sitting on a bench by the front door in the twi-
light, discussing the situation in low voices,
were unaware that every little bush, every
clump of grass, concealed an armed enemy.

The animals knew that Freddy was a prisoner
in the house, but they didn't know where, and
they certainly couldn't rescue him while the
two men were around. So some of the Horribles
crawled into the house and closed the front door
with a bang and turned the key. And at this sig-

nal the skunks rose up behind their grass clumps and commenced shooting. *Whit, whit, whit* went the arrows. They didn't make any noise when they hit Mr. Condiment but Mr. Condiment made plenty. So did Mr. Newsome. "Ouch! Oh-ouch! Oh ow-yow-yow!" It was hard to tell which yelled the loudest as they dashed at the door. They shoved and they tugged at the doorknob and pushed each other aside and howled, and all the time the arrows, some tipped with wire and some with porcupine quills, were going *whit, whit, whit* into their backs and legs. At last Mr. Newsome woke up to the fact that the door was locked. He turned and dashed off down the old road towards his car, and the archers let him go. And then Sniffy unlocked the door and pulled it quickly open, and Mr. Condiment plunged in and fell flat on his face in the hall, looking in the dimness, with the dozens of little arrows sticking in him, like an enormous porcupine.

The animals swarmed in after him and Sniffy locked the door again. Mr. Condiment made no effort to get up; he just lay and groaned.

"Where have you hidden Freddy?" Sniffy demanded.

"Oh-oh-oh!" Mr. Condiment moaned.

So Sniffy motioned to the others and they began pulling the arrows out of him. Of course they hadn't gone into him more than quarter of an inch, but porcupine quills have little barbs on them and they hurt a lot more coming out than they do going in. Mr. Condiment yelped every time one was pulled out. And at last he said: "Oh cease, desist—I mean, stop! You're killing me."

"Foul caitiff loon!" said Sniffy. "We slay thee not yet. But an thou tellest not where thou hast hidden Freddy, that great and noble pig, we give thee fair warning—these arrows which we have withdrawn from thy measly hide we will shoot back into thee, and so will continue, to withdraw, and then shoot them—"

"Oh, here—here!" Mr. Condiment groaned. "In the closet off the kitchen." And he pulled the key out of his pocket.

When they had released Freddy he hobbled out into the hall—for he was pretty stiff—and lit a lamp. Then he looked on Mr. Condiment. "Good work, Sniffy," he said. "Not much fight left in him." He grinned. "I heard your little speech. Thanks for the 'great and noble.' "

"Oh, well," said the skunk. "That was Robin Hood talk. You don't have to take it literally."

"Nay, lad," Freddy said, "'tis thou that deservest the praise. Thou hast captured this great beast, and tonight in thy honor shall the feast be spread. Let great fires be lit, and we will e'en roast him and devour him to the last whisker."

People who read comics will believe almost anything, and Mr. Condiment had of course read, and no doubt enjoyed, a great many. With some difficulty he sat up and stared wildly around at the armed skunks, and the strange looking Horribles, with their ears pinned down and little tin knives flashing in their paws. He had no doubt that their threat to cook and eat him would be carried out. He got to his knees and began to beg for his life.

Freddy was disgusted with him. "Oh, keep still," he said. "You, Junior, pull the rest of those arrows out of his back." And when this had been done to an accompaniment of squeals: "We've got to lock him up so those other two won't find him when they come back. Where's Mr. Newsome?"

"I followed him to his car," said No. 7. "He

jumped in and drove off. Guess he's had enough."

They decided that the only place to hide Mr. Condiment was under the floor in the kitchen. The hole the skunks had dug from the outside was too small for him to escape through. They made him walk into the kitchen and lie down in the space where the board was pulled up.

"Hadn't we ought to tie him up and gag him?" 18 asked.

"I kind of hate to do that," Freddy said. "Though after they come back, if he starts yelling or banging on the floor . . ."

"I can fix it," said Sniffy. He put his head down in the hole. "Petey!" he said. "Hey, Pete! Come here a minute."

Presently a brown centipede crawled up over the edge of the hole. "Hi, skunk. What's on your mind?" he said. He had a harsh, rather unpleasant voice—though of course quite small.

"We want this guy to lie quiet under here for a while," Sniffy said. "So if he starts to yell or make any noise, maybe you and the boys would warn him to shut up. Walk around on his face, maybe, or crawl up his pant leg."

"Sure, sure," said Pete. "Give him the old pincers, eh?"

"Oh, no rough stuff. No, just a warning."

"O K," said the centipede. "He won't give you any trouble. But I'll just drop him a hint. A stitch in time, you know." He went down and walked up Mr. Condiment to his shoulder and whispered something in his ear. "Ugh!" said Mr. Condiment and shuddered.

Freddy leaned over the opening. "I don't like doing this, Mr. Condiment," he said, "But I warn you, we'll do much worse things if you don't quit picking on Mademoiselle Rose."

"Yah!" Mr. Condiment jeered. But it was a weak jeer; his heart wasn't in it.

So they put back the board and Freddy found a hammer and nails and nailed it down.

"How'd you ever manage to get friendly with that thousand-legger, Sniffy?" he asked. "They're usually sort of stand-offish."

"Sniffy has a great talent for making friends," said Aroma admiringly.

"Don't I know it! That no-good sneak, Lyman, is one of 'em. And by the way, if Lyman came up with Newsome, he must be around somewhere. And so must Jinx. We'd better find them both before the plane gets back."

CHAPTER
15

"Talk about dilemmas!" said Freddy. "We're in a dandy. We've got Condiment, but what can we do with him? If my plane was here—"

"Which it isn't," put in Sniffy.

"No, and when it comes back those men will come with it, and they've got guns. And we can't keep Condiment there under the floor more than a few hours. Oh, sure—he did it to me. I'll put him in jail if I can, but we mustn't be cruel."

"Can't we go down to West Nineveh and get the state troopers to arrest him?" 18 asked.

"What for? Locking up a pig in a closet? Burning down a barn? It's probably his own barn. Trying to marry Mademoiselle Rose? That's no crime."

"We can prove he tried to ruin Mr. Boom," said 18.

"How?" Freddy asked. "I don't believe we could prove anything against him now that his plane's burned up. No, the police can't help us; we've got to do it all ourselves."

"Like Robin Hood," Sniffy said.

"That's right. We've got to get rid of these two, Jackson and Felix, and then we've got to get rid of Condiment. Darn it, you know I almost did get rid of him; if I could have worked that Leopard Woman stuff on him a few more times, I think he would have quit. Now that's all spoiled by my own carelessness." He sighed

and covered his eyes with his right fore trotter,
but he peeked out to see if anybody was going
to say: "Oh, no, no! You've done wonders!" But
nobody did.

Two of the Horribles came hopping in the
door. "No. 11 reporting," said one of them. "No
sign of either Jinx or Lyman, Your Dreadfulness. We've covered the whole farm and the
woods. Muskrat tracks where the car was
parked; we think he went back with Mr. Newsome."

"Well, that's that," said Freddy. "I suppose
the plane may be back any time now. Hope they
don't crash it, landing. But that Jackson must
know all his landmarks, and my plane has got
landing lights. Oh, golly, maybe it would be
better if they did crash. We could handle Condiment if we had him alone. Hey, wait a minute!" he said suddenly. "I wonder if they know
Condiment's hand-writing. Oh well, I can fix
that."

He went over to the table and took a pencil
and wrote on a sheet of paper:

"Jackson: Hope you can read this. I fell and
hurt my right hand. Newsome has driven me
down to see a doctor. We have disposed of the

pig. As soon as you get back, take Felix with you and go up into the woods at the north of the house and see if you can find out what is going on. We saw lights and heard voices.

                                     Condiment."

"There," Freddy said as he pinned his note to the front door; "now when they come back we ought to have a chance to get Condiment into the plane and I can fly him down to the farm. After that, we'll see."

There was nothing the matter with the scheme except, as Sniffy said later, that it didn't work. It was after midnight when the plane came back. Freddy had hidden in one of the upstairs rooms, so that when the men left to explore the woods, he would lose no time in getting Mr. Condiment out from under the floor and hustling him down to the plane. There was nothing in the room but twenty or thirty big sacks of flour—evidently for Jackson to use in bombing the circus—and Freddy had tried to make a sort of bed of them but he had only been able to doze uncomfortably.

Freddy heard the plane land, then the men came into the house. He could hear them talking for a minute or so, arguing about something, then the voices grew louder, and he knew that they had come into the kitchen, which was directly below the room he was in.

"Well, if you want to go out and stumble around in the woods, go on," Jackson was saying. "I'm going to make some coffee."

"Yeah, I guess the woods can wait," Felix said. "Say, do you suppose this gadget really works?"

Condiment says it flickers when it goes over metal," Jackson replied. "Here, let me try. I'll try with this quarter." There was a rattle as the coin hit the floor, then after a minute: "Hey, look!" said Jackson. "Sure, it flickers every time I move over the money.—But hold on; it flickers over here, too. A lot brighter than over the quarter. But there's no metal here."

"Let's see," said Felix. And then: "Must be something there. Must be under the floor. Let's pull up this board."

"Oh, golly!" said Freddy.

There was the harsh squeak of nails being pulled out, then: "The boss!" Felix exclaimed. "Why, it's the boss!"

"Of course it's me," said Mr. Condiment's voice. "Get me out of here, you idiots!"

"Sure, sure. But why didn't you holler?" Jackson asked.

"These insects, these thousand-leggers—I mean, these centipedes. They attacked me. Even my nose! Look at it; is the skin broken?"

"Looks the same as usual," said Jackson, and Felix muttered under his breath: "Centipedes punchin' him in the nose! He's gone goofy on us!"

But Mr. Condiment overheard him. "Be quiet, you nincompoop, you blatherskite—I mean, you ninnyhammer! As long as you work for me, you'll—"

"Yeah, I'll what?" Felix interrupted. "Don't know as I want to work for a man that fights centipedes. I'll—"

"Oh, shut up, Felix," said Jackson. "Look, boss, this note you wrote—"

"I didn't write any note. Let's see it. . . . That pig must have written it. He wanted to get you out of the house. Well, he's upstairs somewhere. We'll go up and get him."

The footsteps clattered up the stairs. Freddy pulled one of the sacks of flour into the middle of the room and ripped it open. When the three men came in and turned a flashlight on him, he was bending over the open sack with both fore trotters buried deep in the flour, as if hastily trying to hide something.

"Hold it!" said Jackson. "Don't move. What have you got there?"

"Nothing," said Freddy. "Er . . . nothing. I was just—well, I was just seeing what was in this sack."

They closed in around him, bending over to look.

"He's got something there," said Mr. Condiment. "Careful, it may be a gun. Felix, you—"

It was at that moment, when the three faces were close to the open sack, that Freddy closed his eyes, held his breath, and brought his fore trotters up with a rush through the flour, so that the fine white powder went into the eyes and noses and mouths of the men, blinding them and making them cough and sneeze. Three times he dipped into the sack and threw out flour, until the room was filled with a choking white cloud through which nothing could be seen but a faint glow from the flashlight. Then as he could hold his breath no longer, Freddy dove for the door. He tripped one man, kicked another, and punched the third—he thought it was Mr. Condiment—and then he found the door and got out, slamming it behind him.

It was dark out in the hall, but there was clean air there. He drew some long breaths and then started down the stairs. He would have liked to stay and listen, for now the men were fighting among themselves. Blinded and half choked, they supposed at first that Freddy was still in the room, for they had tried to return his blows and had hit one another. They blundered about, swinging wildly at anyone who came near them, but with every breath they drew in more flour, so that they coughed and wheezed, and at last had to stop fighting and groped feebly for the door. But by the time they were outside, Freddy was running for his plane.

But he heard them stumbling down the stairs, and he knew he wouldn't have time to start the engine and climb in and get away. So he stopped and hid behind a tree, and when they came pounding past him, he doubled back, went into the house again, and closed and locked the door.

A few minutes later Sniffy and No. 18 came in through the hole under the house. "What do we do now, Freddy?" Sniffy asked. "Golly, they scared us into fits when they came out the front door. All covered with white—we thought they were ghosts. But how did they find old Condiment? We didn't hear him bang on the floor or yell or anything."

"The Piggy Bank," Freddy said. "They were trying it, and of course when it went over him, it lit up."

"I don't see why," 18 said. "He certainly isn't solid gold. Or even nickel."

"Probably has some change in his pocket," said Freddy. "That's what did it. Well now, look, 18. Send in enough of your Horribles to give us a sentry at each window. Because Condiment will try to get in and get the bank. We'll be in a state of siege all right, but we only need enough garrison to keep watch; we can't do much fighting. If the rest of you stay outside, maybe you can discourage them, if they attack."

Freddy didn't have much hope that they could beat off a determined attack. There were two guns left in the house but he couldn't find any ammunition. There were of course the two guns, and shells, in the hollow tree beyond the barn, but they couldn't get them across and into

"They scared us into fits—all covered with white."

the house without being caught. Freddy was scared. "Golly," he said, "here I am trying to get Mr. Boom out of a dilemma, and I get into a worse one myself. If the Frederick & Wiggins Dilemma Service can't do any better than this, it ought to go out of business."

"You'll be out of business quick if Condiment gets in here," said Sniffy. He looked sharply at Freddy. "Nay, look not so downcast, lad," he said. "Hast ever known a Wilson to flinch from the fight? We'll stand by thee to the last skunk."

As Sniffy had intended it made Freddy grin. "Oh, sure," he said. "And I'll fight to the last pig. Only I *am* the last pig. That's not so good."

"They're coming to the front door," No. 6 called from the window. And at once there was a heavy knock.

"Open up, pig!" Jackson shouted.

CHAPTER

16

Freddy's tail had come uncurled; it always did when he was scared. When Jackson shouted the second time for him to open up, he tried to think of something to say in reply, something defiant, and insulting without being vulgar. But he was afraid that his voice might squeak, as it sometimes did when he was excited and also he couldn't think of anything. So he kept still and peered out through the little window at the side of the door.

Jackson and Felix were close to the door and Mr. Condiment stood behind them—a poor place to be, as it turned out. They were still white with flour. Freddy saw Jackson hold the lantern higher, and Felix raised a short axe and drove it in to split the door panel. At the same moment three little clouds of flour dust puffed out from the back of Mr. Condiment's coat and with a loud screech he turned and ran. Felix and Jackson swung round. "I don't like this," said Felix. "First he claims centipedes are chasin' him, and now this! Guy's gone nuts."

"Maybe so," said Jackson. "But we want that gadget." And he raised the axe again.

And three little puffs of dust came out of *his* coat, and he said: "Ouch!" and whirled around and followed Mr. Condiment.

"Well for gosh sakes!" said Felix. He held up the lantern and looked after his friend. Then evidently he caught sight of the two arrows sticking in Jackson's back. He dropped the lantern and began beating on the door. "Hey, pig!" he shouted. "Let me in! Save me! My gosh, if I'd known there was Indians up in this country I'd never have left Philadelphia. Hey, don't leave us out here to be murdered! Let me in!"

Freddy didn't answer. But some of the Horribles hiding out in the grass had heard, and they lifted up their voices in a pretty good imitation of a war whoop. Felix dropped the lantern and ran. They could hear him crashing through the brush on the south side of the field. Slowly the sound died away. "He'll be back in Philadelphia by morning at that rate," Freddy said. And perhaps he was. At any rate, he was never seen again in that part of the country.

But Jackson was made of sterner stuff. Half an hour later he came back. He had on a heavy leather jacket which the little arrows could not pierce and he had tied newspapers around his legs and arms. Condiment was with him, but stayed well in the background while he again attacked the door. But this time Freddy was ready for him. For the window over the front door had been opened and a sack of flour balanced on the sill. And at the first blow of the axe Freddy dumped the contents of the sack on his head. Blinded and choking, he stumbled down from the steps and Mr. Condiment led him away.

One more attempt however the enemy made that night to force an entrance into the house. They attacked the back door. They came with a rush, down through the woods which grew close to the house on that side, carrying between them a length of two by four with which they hoped to smash in the lock at the first impact. And perhaps they would have succeeded. But just before they reached the house there was a flash and a tremendous bang among the trees behind them, and shot rattled on the clapboards. Somebody had fired a shotgun at them. They dropped the two by four and ran.

It was the Horribles who had had the honor of repelling this last charge. Eight of them had taken one of the guns from the hollow tree and had dragged it across the field and up back of the house, where they had got it up on to an old stump so that the muzzle was pointing at the door. It was 23 who had pulled the trigger. Some time later his comrades brought him into the house on an improvised litter. The gun of

It was 23 who had pulled the trigger.

course had kicked him so hard that he had turned two complete somersaults, and he had a badly sprained shoulder and was suffering from shock. It was for this brave deed that he later got the Benjamin Bean Distinguished Service Medal.

After this there were no further attacks on the house and presently No. 4 came in to report that the men had climbed into the plane and gone to sleep. "Condiment wanted Jackson to fly him back to Philadelphia to get reinforcements," he said, "but Jackson said he'd been up all night and was too tired—he had to sleep first. And anyway, he said, he didn't need any reinforcements. He said no pig could put anything over on him. He said, wait till morning, he'd get into the house all right."

"He can, too," said Freddy. "They've got pistols. I guess we'll have to abandon the house. If we hide in the woods—"

"Rabbit No. 4 reporting," said a voice from the doorway. "There's a car coming up the old road. Jackson's gone out to stop it. He took a pistol."

"Come on," said Freddy. He unlocked the front door cautiously and went out. It was beginning to get light. In the fringe of trees at the edge of the field he stopped. A car started somewhere, and then a station wagon came slowly across to the plane. Jackson walked beside it. It drew up beside the plane, but Freddy couldn't hear what was being said. After a few minutes Jackson got into the wagon and it drove off.

Pretty soon No. 4 came back. "They were lost," he said. "Got on the wrong road. Mr. Condiment asked them to take Jackson down to West Nineveh so he could phone to Mr. Mandible, in Philadelphia. He is to tell Mandible to charter a plane and come at once. He said to bring guns."

"Well, he's alone in the plane," Freddy said, "but we can't do anything when he's armed. I guess we're stuck. Who were those people, 4?"

"Little man with a black beard was driving. And there was a great big woman in the back. She had on a hat—gosh, I never saw such a big hat. She did all the talking. Very deep voice, she had. Funny thing, it sounded familiar, too. Reminded me of somebody I know, but I couldn't for the life of me tell who."

Freddy went back in and got the Benjamin

Bean Improved Self-filling Piggy Bank and they took it up in the woods and hid it. Then he moved down to a position near the burned-out barn, where he could watch the plane. It was daylight now. Mr. Condiment's head was sticking up out of the rear cockpit, peering around in all directions like a hen in a crate. There was nothing to be done, so Freddy lay down on the ground and went to sleep.

Perhaps an hour later Sniffy woke him. "Car's coming." He got up and went to the edge of the road and watched from behind a tree. The car crawled along over the ruts. "They haven't got Jackson," said Sniffy.

Freddy could see the people in the car now. The woman in the back seat was enormous; he couldn't figure how she had ever managed to get in. She was wrapped and swathed in shawls and she had on a hat which reminded him of the White Queen in *Alice,* only it was bigger. It stuck way out at the sides and a veil was draped over it and over her big white face—the kind of voluminous veil that women used to wear in the early days of automobiles, when there weren't any windshields.

Freddy stepped out into the road, and the car stopped. "Well, young man?" said the woman in a deep booming voice.

"Excuse me," said Freddy. "May I speak to you a moment?"

"That's what you're doing, ain't it?" she said. "Not that I want to hear anything you've got to say. Stand aside, young whippersnapper, if you don't want to be run over. Drive on, Percival."

The driver jerked his head around and stared at her; then he muttered something and shifted gears.

But Freddy stood his ground. "Wait a minute. That man in there, Mr. Condiment—he's a crook. He's a—"

"And what are you, may I ask?" she boomed. "Well, I'll answer that myself. I know you! You're the fat, lazy good-for-nothing pig that lives on poor old Mr. Bean, eating him out of house and home. You're that pig that runs a bank for animals, and gets their money away from them and they never get it back. You're the editor of the Bean Home News that prints terrible lies about your friends and—"

Freddy began to laugh. "Hold it, hold it!" he said. "That's the truth—every word you've spoken is the truth. Now do you want me to tell you who you are?"

"Oh, dear land!" she said. "I knew you'd recognize me, Freddy." And she put back her veil and disclosed the broad face of Mrs. Wiggins. "How do you like this get-up? Think I've got too much lipstick on?"

"I like your hat," Freddy said. "But who's your chauffeur? I don't seem to know him."

The driver unhooked his beard from his ears and rubbed his chin. "Hot," he said. "Wonder how General Grant stood it."

"Uncle Ben!" Freddy exclaimed. "Well, I really didn't know you!"

"Look, Freddy," Mrs. Wiggins said. "We got rid of Jackson down the road a piece. He may go to Nineveh and phone, or he may not. Last we saw of him he was cavortin' off over the hills, yellin', so I'd guess not."

"How'd you get rid of him?" Freddy asked.

Mrs. Wiggins grinned. "Put back my veil and kissed him," she said. "Oh, I mustn't think of it, I'll get to laughing. What do you want me to do?"

"Tell me first what happened. Why you're here," he said.

So she told him that when Mr. Condiment's plane had landed at the farm they had of course thought it was Freddy. The men had come down through the barnyard and gone up into the loft and taken the Benjamin Bean Improved Self-filling Piggy Bank and marched off with it without any opposition at all. A few of the animals had come out, but the men had revolvers—there was nothing to be done. Nobody wanted to call Mr. Bean because they were afraid he'd be shot. But Jinx had come back to the farm with Mr. Condiment—he had hidden in the plane—and he told them about Freddy's capture. "So Uncle Ben and I thought we'd better come up," Mrs. Wiggins said. "So what do you think we'd better do now?"

"That's what I'm going to ask you," Freddy said. "I've messed things up enough. I should stick to detective work and let dilemmas alone."

"Oh, folderol and fiddlesticks!" said Mrs. Wiggins. "You've done plenty. Now let's have your ideas."

Freddy said he hadn't any.

"Good grief!" she said. "If *you've* run out of ideas . . . Well, we'll have to do the best we can with Uncle Ben's. Tell him, Uncle Ben."

Uncle Ben pointed a finger at Mrs. Wiggins. "Demon Woman," he said.

"That's me," said the cow. "You pretty near fixed Condiment with the Great Serpent and the Leopard Woman. Now if the Demon Woman of Grisly Gulch comes alive—well, what are we waiting for? Get in and crouch down, Freddy, so Condiment won't see you." She pulled down her veil. "Drive on, Percival." And Uncle Ben hooked on his beard and started the car.

CHAPTER

17

Uncle Ben drove the station wagon up near the plane and Mr. Condiment climbed out and went over to speak to Mrs. Wiggins. Freddy, crouched down in the rear seat with a blanket over him, heard Mr. Condiment ask where

Jackson was, and Mrs. Wiggins' reply: "My dear sir, I haven't the *faintest* idea! Most extraordinary behaviour! When we arrived at the bus station, he said: 'Let me out here.' And then he said: 'Kiss old Condiment goodbye for me,' and the last we saw of him he was getting into the Utica bus."

"Great heavens!" said Mr. Condiment. "You mean that he didn't telephone?"

"No doubt he will do so when he reaches Utica," said Mrs. Wiggins. "He seemed a most vulgar fellow; you should be happy to be rid of him."

Mr. Condiment shook his head. "I can't understand it. It's most disturbing, perplexing—I mean to say, odd."

Mrs. Wiggins' genteel manner, combined with her deep voice and the emphatic nods with which she punctuated her remarks, had reduced Freddy to a quaking jelly of laughter. Even Uncle Ben shook a good deal and his false beard jigged up and down in a way that must have startled Mr. Condiment if he had noticed it. But he was staring with consternation at Mrs. Wiggins.

"I am at a complete loss to understand it,"

he said. "But I am deeply indebted to you, ma'am. My name is Condiment—Watson P."

Mrs. Wiggins bowed majestically. "Charmed. My own name is perhaps not unknown to you. I am the Countess Chinitzky of New York, Newport and Grisly Gulch, Wyoming."

Mr. Condiment jumped. "Grisly Gulch!" he gasped. "And the Countess Chinitzky! But th-that was the name of the Demon Woman. And Grisly Gulch!"

"I know," said Mrs. Wiggins. "Ridiculous, those old stories. I believe there have even been books written about me. So amusing—just fancy, sir; they accuse me of having horns and a tail!" She began to laugh. "And of devouring my enemies—even men like yourself, sir—eating them whole and swallowing them down, body, boots and breeches." And she laughed harder than ever.

Mrs. Wiggins' laugh was known to every man, woman, child, animal, bird and insect in the north central part of the state. She was now of course two hundred miles from home, but it is possible that some of the better jokes told to Mrs. Wiggins had provoked laughter loud enough to be heard even at that distance. Of course she didn't just laugh at good jokes, she laughed at all of them—good, bad and indifferent. Some of her friends complained of this. "We don't mind hearing you laugh at something really funny," they said. "What we object to is hearing you roar your head off over some old riddle that Noah brought over in the Ark." But Mrs. Wiggins only said that a joke was a joke, and old ones, that had stood the test of time, were the best. "I don't like to have to figure out what the point is," she said. "When you've heard a joke fifteen or twenty times, you know just when to laugh. Although," she would add thoughtfully, "I like to laugh at 'em whether I get the point or not."

Mr. Condiment felt terribly alone as that great roaring laughter beat down on him. First Newsome, then Felix, and now Jackson had deserted him. And on top of that—well, the Great Serpent had been bad, Lorna the Leopard Woman had been horrible. But now this, the Ghost of Grisly Gulch in person! It was just too much. He leaned weakly against the side of the station wagon and moaned.

And Mrs. Wiggins stopped laughing. "Well,

sir," she said, "I fear we must be getting on. So I will just carry out your man Jackson's request and kiss you goodbye." She took off her hat and then leaned out and put her front hoofs on Mr. Condiment's shoulders. Jinx had made her up with burnt cork eyebrows and powdered her with lots of flour, and when Mr. Condiment saw that huge white face coming close to his own, with the horns and the big flat teeth in a mouth large enough to snap his head off at one bite, he gave a little yelp and dropped his pistol and sank to the ground. There was no fight left in him and they had no further trouble with him. They helped him into the house and gave him a drink of water, and then Freddy sat him down at the table with pen and paper and said: "Now write as I dictate.

"I, Watson P. Condiment, being of sound mind, but pretty well scared by thinking about my crimes, do hereby confess . . ." And Freddy had him write out a full account of his persecution of Mademoiselle Rose and his attempts to ruin Mr. Boomschmidt. He confessed to having his men steal the Benjamin Bean Improved Self-filling Piggy Bank, and indeed he got so inter-

. . . dropped his pistol and sank to the ground.

ested in writing these things down that he confessed to several crimes that Freddy didn't know
anything about.

So then they started for home—Mrs. Wiggins
and Uncle Ben and the Self-filling Piggy Bank
in the station wagon, and Freddy and Mr. Condiment and the Horribles—complete with umbrellas—in the plane. Sniffy and his family decided not to go with them. "You just leave us
here, Freddy," Sniffy said. "Oh, we'll get back
to the Bean farm some day. But we're going to
stay up here in the woods for a while.—I mean,
there be adventures to be sought in the greenwood—yea, belike dragons to be slain and foul
oppressors to be overcome. We like not the tame
life of farm and barnyard. Farewell, lad, we will
see thee anon." He grinned. "Be seeing you,
Countess," he said to Mrs. Wiggins. "Come
lads." And the skunks trooped after him into
the shadow of the forest.

Freddy flew straight to the farm. The Horribles had never been up in a plane in daylight,
and they thought that the country they passed
over ought to look like the maps they had seen,
with each county a different color. "How can
you tell where you are," they wanted to know,

"without any names on the towns?" It took
Freddy nearly a week after they got back to explain it to them, and some of the less bright
ones, like No. 13, are still puzzling over it.

Freddy flew straight to the fair grounds and
marched Mr. Condiment in through the gate
and into the big tent where Mr. Boomschmidt
was rehearsing a new act—a turtle who could
turn cartwheels and back flips. As soon as he
saw them Mr. Boomschmidt rushed up to Mr.
Condiment with his hand outstretched. "My
goodness, if it isn't my old friend—" Then he
stopped. "No, no, of course you're not my
friend," he said: "You're an enemy. Well,
you're welcome just the same, and we'll try to
make you feel at home." The circus animals,
having watched Freddy's arrival, had come
trooping into the tent. "Now here's an old
friend of yours," Mr. Boomschmidt went on.
"Willy, come shake hands with Mr. Condiment."

The boa constrictor came gliding up.
"Haven't got any hands to shake with," he said,
"but I'll be glad to give him a little hug." He
threw a loop around Mr. Condiment. "My, my,
he's the one that's doing the shaking."

"That's enough, Willy," said Mr. Boomschmidt, who saw that Mr. Condiment was not only trembling but had turned a rather muddy green color. "That's *enough!*" he repeated firmly, as Willy began to squeeze. "Go sit down. Do you hear me?—*sit down!*"

That is a pretty hard order for a snake to obey. Willy unwound from Mr. Condiment and looked around helplessly.

"If you don't mind me—!" said Mr. Boomschmidt threateningly.

"Oh, gosh!" said the snake. "Look, chief, you know I can't sit down. Any more than you can glide."

"I can too glide," Mr. Boomschmidt retorted. He took off his silk hat and put it on the ground. "Look here."

"Just a second, Mr. Boom," Freddy said. He would have liked to see Mr. Boom imitate a snake; he was sure it would be pretty instructive; but he wanted to dispose of his prisoner. "Just look at this." And he held out the paper on which Mr. Condiment had written his confession.

Mademoiselle Rose had come into the tent, and she looked over Mr. Boomschmidt's shoul-

der as he read. "Oh dear!" she said. "Oh, dear!"
And after a minute she began to cry quietly.

Mr. Boomschmidt went on reading, but he
kept glancing at her, and when he came to the
bottom of the page he folded the paper up and
handed it back to Freddy. "I guess that settles our what-do-you-call-it, dilemma," he said.
"We'll take him down to the jail and turn him
over to the sheriff." Then he turned to Mademoiselle Rose. "Guess you're coming down with
a cold," he said, whipping out a huge red and
blue checked handkerchief and holding it to
her nose. "Here. Blow!"

She slapped his hand away. "I am not!" she
said angrily, and then she seized the handkerchief and wiped her eyes. "I'm crying," she said.

"Crying!" he exclaimed. "Why, goodness
gracious mercy me, Rosie, what for? Leo!
Where are you, Leo? Do *you* know what she's
crying for?"

"Don't know, chief," said the lion. "Unless
maybe she's sorry for old Condiment here. Going off to jail now, and after all, it's just because
she didn't want to marry him. My old Uncle
Ajax used to say that—"

"Oh, you and your Uncle Ajax go fall off a

cliff!" said Rose furiously, and the other animals all sort of backed away and stared at her, for they had never seen her lose her temper before. They had never seen her look so pretty, either. "And as for you," she said, turning to Mr. Boomschmidt, "can't you ever figure anything out for yourself? Do you always have to ask that old moth-eaten lion to explain it for you?"

"O boy O boy," said Leo under his breath. "You got a good high cliff handy, Freddy? If so, I feel sort of tempted to take a dive off it right now. Because she'll really get going in a minute. Just between you and me—" he lowered his voice still further—"Uncle Ajax always said it was the quiet ones like our Rose who blew up with the loudest bang when they did blow up."

"Why, Rose," said Mr. Boomschmidt. "This —well, it isn't like you. Why, I didn't know you *could* cry."

"Oh, you didn't!" she snapped. "Well, I guess that's right; you didn't know I was a girl at all; I was just another of your performing animals. Why, you've never even treated me as if I was human!"

For the first time in the years Freddy had known him, Mr. Boomschmidt seemed at a loss for words. "Huh?" he said. "What?" He reached up to push his silk hat back off his forehead as he always did when he was trying to think, but of course the hat wasn't there—it was on the ground. Willy saw the gesture, and picked it up and handed it to his employer, but Mr. Boom-schmidt didn't seem to know what to do with it; he just put it down on the ground again.

Mr. Condiment seemed to have recovered somewhat for he wasn't so green any more. He opened his mouth, and then he hesitated, and then he said: "I always thought you were a fool, Boomschmidt, but now I know it."

"Did you?" said Mr. Boomschmidt mildly. "Well, my goodness, maybe you're right. But let me tell you, it isn't so easy to be a fool nowa-days, what with all this education they give you. Not that I ever . . ." His voice trailed off, and evidently he wasn't much interested in what he was saying. He looked helplessly at Leo, but the lion, after a glance at Mademoiselle Rose, shook his head, as much as to say: "Leave me out of this, chief."

"I'd like to propose an agreement, an under-standing—that is, a bargain with you, Boom-schmidt," said Mr. Condiment.

"A bargain? Gracious, there are always two sides to a bargain, aren't there, and you haven't got any side now." Mr. Boomschmidt looked puzzled. "Maybe when you get out of jail, in eight or ten years, we might discuss it, but not now."

Mr. Condiment shivered at mention of jail, but he didn't give up. "Let me ask you a question," he said. "Are you happy?"

"Happy?" said Mr. Boomschmidt. "Of course I'm happy. Leo, don't you think—" He stopped abruptly. "Never mind, Leo," he said. "Just go over back of Hannibal, will you, so I can't see you?"

Leo winked at Freddy and went.

"Well then, you're happy," Mr. Condiment continued. "But you could be happier, couldn't you?"

"Why, I suppose so," said Mr. Boomschmidt. "Goodness, you can always be more of anything. At least I think you can. Tired? Yes, you can be tireder. Sleepy, sunburned, hungry—yes, I can't think of anything you can't be more of. No, my goodness, wait a minute. How about asleep? You can't be asleeper. And—"

"Quite so," said Mr. Condiment. "Well then,

suppose I tell you something that would make you immensely, tremendously—that is to say, a great deal happier. In exchange for that would you be willing to let me go?"

The animals all began to laugh, but Mr. Boomschmidt held up his hand. "Quiet! Why, Mr. Condiment, nothing you have ever said or done up to now has ever made me any happier," he said, "so I kind of doubt—"

Mr. Condiment interrupted him. "Please! I am not proposing that you give me back the confession that I wrote out. You can keep that, so that if I ever give you any trouble in the future you can have me arrested. All I ask is that you do not have me arrested *now*. In case you agree that I have made you happier by what I tell you."

"Oh, I don't have to listen to all this foolishness!" Mademoiselle Rose exclaimed. She gave Rajah, who was standing behind her, a shove that nearly knocked him over, and ran from the tent.

"Oh dear," Mr. Boomschmidt said. "Another dilemma!"

"If you ask me, chief," said Leo, who had come closer now that Rose has left, "it isn't any dilemma, it's just a plain darned mess. Hadn't I better go get the sheriff?"

Mr. Boomschmidt appealed to Freddy. "What do you think about this business? Shall I make a deal with him?"

Freddy wished that Mrs. Wiggins was there. He knew that here was something that needed common sense, and not bright ideas. If he had any common sense, he wondered, what would he do? He thought a minute, and then he said: "Well, I don't see how it can do any harm. If you decide that it does make you happier, you can let him go. You can always put him in jail if he gives you any more trouble. And in a way I'd be sorry to see him locked up in that jail for a long time. Because the sheriff runs an awful nice jail. The prisoners are all happy and contented—goodness, they have ice cream for dessert every night. And I don't think they'd like Mr. Condiment much. He just wouldn't fit in with all those nice burglars, and there'd be trouble right away."

Mr. Boomschmidt picked up his hat and put it on his head. "All right," he said. "I agree, Condiment. What can you tell me?"

"Mademoiselle Rose wants to marry you," Mr. Condiment said.

"What?" Mr. Boomschmidt exclaimed. "You're crazy, Condiment."

The other shook his head. "No, I'm not. She always told me she was in love with somebody else. I thought it was just an excuse, until today." Now I know it wasn't."

"Foolishness!" Mr. Boomschmidt exclaimed. "Why, I'm just a little fat circus man in a fancy vest and Rose is—she is—"

"Why don't you go ask her?" Mr. Condiment said.

Mr. Boomschmidt stared at him for a minute, then he turned and ran out of the tent. His hat fell off, but he didn't stop for it.

Nobody said anything. The animals all stood around in a circle looking at Mr. Boomschmidt's hat. Finally Hannibal said: "You think she wants to marry him?"

"What makes you think *he* wants to marry *her?*" Leslie asked. "Oh, she's pretty and she's nice, but after all, she's only a girl."

The animals didn't pay much attention to Leslie, for alligators are seldom very experienced in affairs of the heart. They are not at all emotional.

"Well, in the meantime, let's lock this guy up," said Leo. So they took Mr. Condiment and locked him up in an empty hyena cage. And for a long time they all stood around in front of the cage and made remarks about him. But Freddy remembered the time Mr. Condiment had slapped his face. "I suppose I ought to give him those slaps back, now I've got the chance," he thought. "But I just can't do it. I know something I can do, though." So he went down to the monkeys' cage and borrowed a big stack of comics. Monkeys are great readers of comics. And he pushed them through the bars of the cage. "Here," he said to Mr. Condiment; "Here's something for you to read." And Mr. Condiment took one look at them and groaned and turned away and buried his face in his hands.

But pretty soon somebody on the edge of the crowd said: "Here they come!" And they saw Rose and Mr. Boomschmidt coming towards them, arm in arm, and beside them, Madame Delphine and Mr. Boomschmidt's mother. Old Mrs. Boomschmidt was sobbing right out loud, so they knew everything was all right, for she always cried when she was happy. The animals started cheering, but Freddy took one look at Mr. Boomschmidt's face, which was smiling so hard that his eyes had almost disappeared, and then he went and opened the door of the hyena cage. "Beat it!" he said. And Mr. Condiment got out and walked away without a word. He never turned his head, and he walked out of the big tent and out of the fair grounds, and for all anybody knows, he walked right off the map, for nobody ever saw him again.

So the next day was the wedding, and all Centerboro was there, as well as all the animals from the circus and from the Bean farm. Mr. Bean, in a long-tailed coat which he hadn't had on since his own wedding, gave the bride away, and Mrs. Wiggins, Mrs. Wurzburger and Mrs. Wogus were the matrons of honor, with big bouquets. And after the ceremony there was a grand party. Music was provided by Freddy who sang several songs of his own composition, accompanying himself on his guitar, and by Mr. Beller and Mr. Rohr, who sang some duets, just slightly off key, like most duets. Later there was dancing.

Mr. Boomschmidt wandered through the crowd beside Rose, wearing a smile so wide that nobody could understand anything he said. Rose hugged Freddy, and she hugged Rajah and Harrison and she even hugged Willy, who cried a little because hardly anybody ever wants to hug a snake. She didn't hug Hannibal, because nobody can hug an elephant successfully, but she patted his shoulder. And she kissed Mrs. Wiggins and Mrs. Wurzburger and Mrs. Wogus on their big broad noses. But when she came to Leo she gave him a special hug. "Oh, Leo," she said. "I'm so ashamed of the horrid things I said to you. Will you forgive me?"

"Why, dye my hair pea green, Rose," he said. "I knew you didn't mean anything. Besides you've done me a big favor." And when she asked him how, he said: "By marrying the chief. Because now when he wants to mix somebody up by asking them questions, instead of asking them to unmanageable animals like me he'll ask you."

"Asking unmanageable animals unanswerable questions, eh?" said Mr. Boomschmidt. "That's what you think I like to do, is it, Leo? Goodness gracious, now I'll have somebody that can really answer the questions, which is more than you've ever done. Eh, Leo, isn't that so? I mean—isn't that so, Rose?"

"I'm not going to answer that one," Rose said.

Mr. Boomschmidt started to say something, and Leo knew by the expression on his face that the chief was going to try to mix him up. But he remembered the Robin Hood talk and decided it would be a good time to try it. "Why, how now, master," he said quickly, "dost thou truly think so ill of my wisdom that thou seekest to rid thyself of my services? Nay, full well thou knowest that I have ever given thee free and fair answers to all thy questionings, and no lack of ripe wisdom thereto. But an thou wilt cast me off, then a murrain seize thee, say I. And indeed I do pity that fair lass there beside thee. Though I warrant she'll e'en answer thy questions in better sort than ever I did. Belike with a sound buffet on thy ear. But thou—"

Mr. Boomschmidt stared at Leo, and his eyes got rounder and rounder, and he pushed his hat back on his head, and grabbed Rose by the arm. "Oh, my gracious! Do you hear that, Rose? Oh, my goodness gracious me! What a line of talk!

No indeed, Leo, you're going to be right beside me next time I get in an argument with anybody, but anybody! Oh *oh,* what a pity old Condiment has gone! What we couldn't have done to mix him up! Here, wait a minute, here comes Freddy. We'll try it on him."

But it didn't work so well with Freddy for he could talk Robin Hood talk too. The result was that for the first time since Leo had known him, Mr. Boomschmidt himself got mixed up, and it was lucky for him that at that minute old Mrs. Peppercorn came up, and Rose had to thank her for the hand-painted umbrella stand she had given them as a wedding present.

Everybody had a wonderful time, and ate a lot too much, but perhaps old Mrs. Boomschmidt had the best time of anybody, for she was so happy that she cried steadily for twenty-four hours. And Uncle Ben, who had taken a great fancy to her, sat beside her and wiped away her tears with a series of large clean pocket handkerchiefs.

Late that night, after the party was over, Freddy flew back home. He was too excited and too happy to sleep, so he lit his lamp, and sat down at his desk and started to write the book which later gained him so much fame. This is what he wrote:

THE SKY IS THE LIMIT.
A Book on Flying for Animals.

The first paragraph, as you probably know, begins:

"No longer is it only birds and men who have the freedom of the great and glorious open spaces of the sky. You too, animals—you pigs and horses and cows and dogs—you too can leave the earth behind, can climb through the clouds and hop the mountain tops, and coast down the sunbeams. Listen . . ."

A NOTE ON THE TYPE

The text of this book was set on the Linotype in Baskerville. Linotype Baskerville is a facsimile cutting
from type cast from the original matrices of a face de-
signed by John Baskerville. The original face was the
forerunner of the "modern" group of type faces.

John Baskerville (1706-75), of Birmingham, England,
a writing-master, with a special renown for cutting in-
scriptions in stone, began experimenting about 1750
with punch-cutting and making typographical ma-
terial. It was not until 1757 that he published his first
work. His types, at first criticized, in time were recognized as both distinct and elegant, and his types as well
as his printing were greatly admired.

Freddy Books Published By
The Overlook Press

FREDDY THE DETECTIVE
by Walter R. Brooks
ISBN 978-1-59020-418-4 • $10.99 • PB

Freddy is inspired while reading *The Adventures of Sherlock Holmes* to become a detective. Setting out with his intrepid partner Mrs. Wiggins the cow, he is ultimately challenged to prove that Jinx the cat was framed for murder.

FREDDY THE POLITICIAN
by Walter R. Brooks
ISBN 978-1-59020-419-1 • $9.99 • PB

Freddy, the good-natured pig with a poetic soul, is promoting a campaign to get Mrs. Wiggins the cow elected president of the First Animal Republic. As he himself is an officer in the newly organized First Animal Bank, he has more than a modicum of influence— if he can just figure out how to use it.

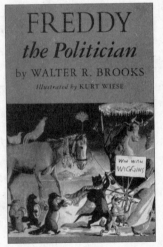

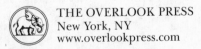
THE OVERLOOK PRESS
New York, NY
www.overlookpress.com